PRICE OF MAGIC

WITCH'S BITE SERIES BOOK TWO

STEPHANIE FOXE

STEEL FOX MEDIA LLC

First edition, September 2017
Version 2.0, May 2019
ISBN 978-1-950310-05-0

Thank you, Michael, for your tireless assistance and endless support. I couldn't have done any of this without you.

Always & Forever

CONTENTS

Four vampires. Three werewolves. That's how many died that night. Avoidable deaths.

That's all I can think about as I stare at the detective across from me who is waiting for an answer to a question he has already asked twice. He's going through everything that happened for the third time, and it's starting to feel like an interrogation.

"You stated that Detective Alexander Novak was able to kill Chevy before succumbing to his wounds?" he repeats, his brows pinched together as he looks down at me over his glasses like I might be too stupid to understand what he just asked.

"Yes," I answer, again. I have to bite the inside of my cheek to keep from adding a 'for the last fucking time'. My hands clench into tight fists where they are tucked under my arms.

Lydia glances at me and shifts to sit up straighter. "This interview has gone on long enough. If you have any other questions, you can refer to my client's written statement. After all, she's a victim here, not a suspect in a murder investigation."

I should be. But I'm not stupid enough to say that aloud, though I wonder what they'd do if I did tell them. It's possible they wouldn't even believe me. No one should be able to do what I can do; it's abnormal even for a witch. My mother had made sure I understood from a young age that if anyone ever found out, my life would be over. I'd be killed or used, and I don't like the idea of either.

I want out of this tiny, cold room and out of the police station. There are too many memories that creep up on me in these places.

"Of course, Ms. Holland." Detective Ross says, his mustache bristling as he purses his lips and nods his head. He stands and thanks each of us. His warm hand is a sharp contrast to my frigid one as we shake.

Lydia leads me out of the room. "Do you mind stopping in to say hello to the police chief? He wanted to apologize in person for Martinez."

I sigh but nod. Turning down the chief's goodwill offering would only lead to me looking bitter. I don't want to have to deal with him ever again, but if I do, I'd rather he remember me fondly.

"Let's just make it quick."

I follow Lydia down the narrow, dingy hall. There are office doors every few feet with little brass nameplates. Most of the doors are closed, but a few are open. A woman with a pixie cut is sitting in one office, feet propped up on a chair. She watches as we walk by, eyes narrowed.

The chief's office is at the end of the hall around a corner. The door is shut, but raised voices are clearly audible from where we stand.

"Your coven member interfered in an ongoing investigation. If that witch hadn't gotten involved, an NWR cell would have stayed active in my damn town! For the last time, McGuinness, your coven's petty bullshit feud with the vampires ends now, or I won't have another witch in this department. I'll report you to both councils if I have to."

McGuinness' response is muffled by the door.

Lydia and I share a look. Her brows are raised, and she's smirking. I can't help smiling as well. I've waited my entire life to hear a coven leader get dressed down like this, and it's just as satisfying as I imagined.

McGuinness went out of his way to make sure I understood I would not be joining his coven as soon as I moved into town. It had almost been enough to run me off before my stubbornness kicked in.

The door flies open, and a red-faced man in a suit that barely stretches across his chest comes barreling out, almost running right into me.

At first he just looks annoyed, but then he recognizes me, and his face turns even redder. He bares his teeth at me, brows furrowed and nostrils flaring. He steps forward, his fingers twitching like he's thinking of casting a spell. I uncross my arms and take a step toward him, holding his gaze. He can fucking try, but it'll be the last thing he does.

Novak's magic is buzzing through me. The coven leader has no idea I have it. I want to fry him to a crisp. I feel a spark on the tip of my finger, then Lydia is jerking me back and getting between us. Sound filters back in, and I realize the chief is shouting at McGuinness again, ordering him out.

McGuinness brushes past Lydia and stomps down the hall without a backward glance, taking the smell of fire with him. My breath is coming uncomfortably fast. The Chief and Lydia are both staring at me, the latter with pinched brows and lips pressed tightly together.

"Olivia, are you all right?" Lydia asks.

"I'm fine," I say, clearing my throat and straightening my jacket.

The chief holds out his hand. "Chief of Police Samuel Timmons. It's good to meet you in person, Ms. Carter."

I shake his hand. "Likewise."

"I intended to apologize for the mishandling of the investigation, but it appears I will also need to apologize for the behavior you just witnessed. I would like to make it clear that I will not be party to the coven's obvious prejudice."

"I appreciate that," I say with a tight smile. "Not your fault he's an ass."

"Do you have a moment to sit down?" Timmons asks, waving back toward his office.

"Sure," I agree.

Lydia tugs my arm to get me to follow Timmons into his office.

His desk is oversized and cluttered. There's a bookshelf behind him filled with awards and pictures of his family, but no books.

"Now, we are still looking for Jason Martinez. We don't have any information yet, which isn't surprising considering his connections. I've been in contact with JHAPI and the Vampire Council. From what I hear, there will be a representative from the Vampire Council coming to town to assist JHAPI with the search if he can."

Joint Human and Paranormal Intelligence are involved? They must be serious. That particular organization hasn't actually been around that long, only six years if I remember right. It was formed after the NWR became a more public problem. It was the first cooperative human and paranormal task force created, and it was a surprising success. The councils are always vying for influence over it, of course, but

JHAPI has been successful in slowing down the NWR over the years despite that.

"Please keep us updated, Chief Timmons. We, of course, will continue to help in any way we can," Lydia says politely.

Timmons pulls two cards out of his desk and scribbles a number on the back of each. "My personal cell number is on the back. Don't hesitate to contact me if you need anything or have any information."

I stand and tuck the card into my jacket. "Thanks."

"We'll be in touch," Lydia says.

I walk out before he can think of anything else to discuss. I'm halfway down the hall before Lydia makes it out of his office. I can hear her hurrying after me, but I don't slow down until I'm in the parking lot.

I lean back against my car and cross my arms. There's a crisp coolness in the air that wasn't there yesterday. The first hint of fall always comes as a surprise to me. Summer seems endless until I walk outside and it smells different, and a breeze raises goosebumps on my arms.

She comes to a stop in front of me. "Will you reconsider staying at the clanhouse for the rest of the week?"

"No, I need to feed my cat and catch up on brewing," I say as I pull my keys out. "I also don't want another night of Javier hovering over me like some kind of creepy mother hen."

Lydia sighs, but her lips curl up into a smile. She had laughed at me this afternoon after I finally woke up when I had complained. "He means well."

"I know." I gnaw at the inside of my cheek. "How is Patrick?"

"He is not himself yet. Which is why Javier is being so ridiculous. Patrick won't let him hover either."

I roll my eyes. That's the most I've gotten out of her since yesterday morning, and it's not enough.

"You're being vague. Not himself," I mock, throwing up sarcastic finger quotes. "Javier wouldn't let me see him, so something is obviously wrong. Just tell me."

Lydia huffs and shakes her head. "Javier didn't want you to worry, but I suppose that's impossible. Patrick is angry. He has had several outbursts. He almost hurt one of the neckers and did not appreciate the manner in which Javier stopped him. They've been arguing like cats and dogs."

"I want to talk to him."

"Javier has said no visitors since the incident with the necker. He's even having his blood delivered in a cup."

I grimace at the visual. "That's only going to piss Patrick off more. Is he really that out of control?"

"I don't know." Lydia clasps her hands in front her, thumb tapping restlessly against the back of her hand.

I need to see Patrick, but I can't deny the little shiver of fear that accompanies the thought. Especially if he isn't fully back in control. The rational mind has a hard time reconciling that a friend could try to kill you and it is not their fault.

"I'm going to come see him soon, whether Javier likes it or not."

"Just give him one more night, Olivia. I wouldn't ask you that if I didn't think it was best for Patrick too. He's struggling for control right now."

I nod. Lydia's honesty is what I need right now. "Any news on when the council representative is coming? Or why they want to see me specifically?"

"Nothing yet," Lydia sighs. "They won't tell me who they're sending, or when. Javier is preparing for the visit as best he can."

"Do you think I'm in some kind of trouble?"

Lydia taps a finger against her chin, considering.

"Having the council's attention is never a good thing, but I don't think you are in trouble for something you did," she says. "You'll have to be careful, and I know this goes against all your instincts, but please be polite to the representative they send."

I roll my eyes. "I'll be polite if they're polite."

"Olivia, this will not be someone like any of the vampires you've met. They'll be old, and strong, and possibly not willing to deal with any attitude."

"I'll figure it out. Just keep me updated, all right?" I say, crossing my arms. She has no faith in me. I'm not a six-year-old. I can be polite if I need to.

"I'll keep you updated. Oh, that reminds me. Will you still be able to come by for the regular checkups this week?"

"Yes." The return to routine sounds like a nice distraction.

Lydia squeezes my arm gently. "Stay safe, and stay in touch, all right?"

"Sure thing," I say as I slip into my car.

Lydia watches me drive off, her lips one thin line. I must seem worse off than I thought if she's worrying this much.

We spent almost three hours at the police station. The sun is setting now, and since it's a cloudy night, it's magnificent. I roll the windows down and dance my fingers in the brisk wind. Patrick is alive. I'm alive. We won. That should be enough to get this sick feeling out of my stomach.

Yet, all I can think about is how it felt when Novak died. I wasn't even sure it was possible to kill someone just by taking their magic.

I smack the power button on the radio. I have to stop thinking about this; it's not healthy. Avoidance is a much better option. Tequila might work too, but I don't think I have any left.

I sing along with the radio as I drive. Classic rock, then some generic pop when commercials come on. I'm ready to be home. If I can just bury myself in normalcy, maybe I can get this knot of anger in my chest to loosen.

Martinez's face, the skin twisted and burned on one side, seems to be all I can see every time I shut my eyes. That or Laurel Ramirez hanging from the ceiling like a side of meat. Or Patrick with empty eyes and spit dripping from his chin, nothing left but hunger.

I turn down my driveway, finally, and I'm relieved to see everything is as I left it. The kitchen light is on, and the porch is lit up. I park, grab all my things, and hurry to the front door, keys ready. As soon as I open the door, Mr. Muffins is twining between my legs, meowing loudly.

"I know, I know, I'm sorry," I say as I trip my way inside.

She bites my ankle through my pants.

"Ow! Give me a damn second." I dump my keys, gun, and jacket on the table and go to the laundry room to refill her water and food, only to find they're both still half-filled. I turn around and glare at her. She's sitting in the middle of the kitchen, licking her paw.

"Seriously? All that, and you aren't even starving?"

She meows and stalks over to the fridge.

"I see how it is. You miss one day of treats and turn feral," I grumble as I get a can of wet food out of the fridge. Mr. Muffins is aggressively spoiled, and I only have myself to blame.

The can opener is still in the sink from the last time I fed her. I open the can as she paces back and forth behind me.

"Here you go, Princess Butthead," I say as I drop the can on the floor and ruffle the fur on her head. She buries her face in the food and ignores me.

Everything is where I left it, including the pile of dirty clothes in the bathroom and the mess in the workroom. I don't want to deal with any of it. It'll still be here tomorrow anyhow.

There's a knock on the door, and I jump, my heart kicking into overdrive. No one ever visits me. If Javier were having someone dropped off to be healed, I would have gotten a text.

I walk as quietly as I can to the table and grab the gun. I should have just gotten Mr. Muffins and stayed at the clanhouse.

"Olivia?" the person shouts through the door.

I'd know that voice anywhere. It's Patrick.

2

I run to the door and pull it open, the gun forgotten in my other hand. Patrick is standing on the porch, face gaunt, and the blue eyes that should be sparkling with mischief are instead glassy and bloodshot. His hands are tucked into the pockets of his faded blue jeans, and his mouth is a thin line of worry. His usually artfully tousled brown hair is dull and messy. He looks nothing like himself.

"Hey," he says quietly. "Do you think I could stay with you for a while?"

Lydia's warning is ringing in my head, but I can't stop myself from stepping out onto the porch and throwing my arms around him. He hugs back tightly, his body trembling. We stand there for a long moment. I wait until he stops shaking so much to pull back.

"So, is that a yes?" he asks, his mouth twitching up into a forced smile.

"Always," I say, punching him lightly on the arm. His eye flicks to my forearm, and the bandage covering the bite he inflicted and the area the bullet grazed me. The smile fades into a frown. I grab his hand and drag him inside.

Mr. Muffins leaves her food and trots over to him. Patrick is her favorite; she definitely loves him more than me.

"Hey, pretty girl," he says, leaning down to pick her up. She rubs her head against his jaw and purrs so loudly, it sounds like she's growling.

I lean back against the sink and watch him cuddle my cat. The tension is bleeding out of his shoulders as he whispers sweet nothings to her and scratches behind her ears.

"So did you run away or Javier let you out of solitary confinement?" I ask as I grab an old bottle of whiskey out of the cabinet. I shouldn't drink right now, but I need something to relax. It's been one thing after another.

I look back when he doesn't answer. He has his face buried in Muffin's fur, and his shoulders are tight once again. He turns away and walks into the living room, plopping down on the couch.

I sigh and pour too much whiskey into my glass. He can make this as difficult as he wants, but I'm getting answers.

He doesn't scoot away when I sit down shoulder-to-shoulder with him on the couch.

"Seriously, Patrick? You don't have to explain everything, but I need to know if Javier is going to come bust down my door looking for you," I say, nudging his shoulder and reaching over to smooth my fingers through Muffin's fur.

"He won't be looking for me. I've left the clan," Patrick says quietly, his voice monotone.

My hand stills, and I look at him with wide eyes. Leaving a clan isn't something you do lightly; it's like disowning your family.

"What—why?" I stutter over my words.

"Javier is a selfish, idiotic asshole," Patrick says,

eyes flashing. "I will not serve someone who doesn't care about their clan members. It's his fault Emily is dead."

I take a deep breath, then drain my glass. This is a mess, and whatever he and Javier are fighting about seems like it might have been coming for a while. I've never seen Patrick this angry.

"Are you okay?" I ask quietly.

"Not really," he says, staring blankly at his knees.

"Do you have people you can feed on? I can round up some girls if I need to. They know me."

"I'll be fine. I have some neckers that like me. I fed before I came here." His eyes stray to my bandaged arm again.

"It wasn't your fault."

"I wish that made me feel better."

My heart sinks into my stomach, heavy as a stone. I knew it would be like this, and I hate that I can't fix it.

"They were beating me, and she provoked them. She got under Martinez's skin to distract him, and he took a baseball bat to her head. It just split open and..." He stops talking, his voice catching. "She did it to save me. It's my fault she died. I was weak, and I was begging for them to stop and let me feed, and she couldn't stand to watch it anymore."

I pull him into a hug, and he buries his face in my neck as sobs wrack his body. I can't stop the tears that slip out of my eyes.

There's a bright light shining in my eyes. I blink and roll over, and my stomach jerks as I fall. I flail against the blanket I'm tangled in, and my shin hits something hard.

"Ow, fuck." I look around groggily and realize I'm now on the living room floor. I was on the couch before I rolled off it like an idiot.

Patrick. I jerk upright and look around. He's not in the living room, but I don't remember him leaving either.

I disentangle myself and stumble toward my bedroom. The blinds are tightly drawn, and the closet door is shut. I breathe a sigh of relief.

I tiptoe over, even though I know I couldn't wake him now if I tried, and crack open the door. Patrick is curled up in the back corner of the closet with his head on one of my pillows and my fluffy blanket pulled up to his chin. Mr. Muffins is curled up by his head, also fast asleep.

I must have fallen asleep last night after he started watching that show he loves so much. It's a stupid kids' show, but he loves it. He hadn't even cracked a smile last night, but he had stopped sobbing, so I was calling it a win.

He looks peaceful now. I lean down and tuck the blanket a little closer around him. My phone vibrates. I pull it out and see an email notification for a delivered shipment. I frown; what did I order?

"The warehouse?" I mumble as I read the address.

Oh, of course. It seems like I placed the order with Gerard months ago, but it's been less than a week. I shove my phone back in my pocket and slip out of the closet, closing the door carefully behind me. I wanted to talk to Maybelle, so this is just another reason to head into town. It's also almost four pm. I've been on the vampire sleeping schedule since before the attack.

I take a quick shower and braid my wet hair to keep it out of my face. I grab jeans, boots, and a flannel shirt out of the closet, just because it's starting to feel like fall. Mr. Muffins meows at me for disturbing her.

I grab my jacket and make sure I have the right potions in the pockets. Novak's magic is still settling into place inside of me, but I don't feel like I can rely on it yet. The brews make me feel safer. The gun is still sitting on the table, and I almost leave it, but I grab it, just in case. I'll have to leave it in the glovebox since I can't get any kind of carry permit with my record.

Stepping outside doesn't disappoint. It's not cool enough to see my breath, but I do get a chill when the breeze picks up. The paint on the rear of my car is peeling badly now. I really should get it fixed. Maybe I'll be able to afford it once I start selling the medicinal brews.

I climb inside, tuck the gun in the glovebox, and head toward town with the windows down and the radio turned up loud. Leaving Patrick alone makes me nervous, but he's as safe there as he is anywhere else. If the NWR wanted to attack, they're more likely to hit the clanhouse directly anyhow. I shift in my seat and try to push the 'what if's out of my mind.

I don't have to drive past Rudie's to get to the cafe, but I do anyhow. The whole thing is starting to feel like a bad dream, and I need to see that it's real. I park along the street and climb out of my car. Police tape lines the entire area, flickering in the breeze.

The parking lot is empty. Most of the windows have been busted out. It looks like something out of a ghost town or dystopian novel. The sign isn't lit up, and the faint smell of smoke drifts across the parking lot.

No one had any way of knowing what was underneath it. I didn't know when I was eating my burger

STEPHANIE FOXE

and thinking the worst part of my week was going to be seeing Tyler with another girl.

Martinez had seemed so normal. Chevy had too. I don't understand what makes a person build a dungeon under their restaurant and start killing people.

I shake my head and climb back in my car, slamming the door. My tires squeal as I take off, eager to get away from all of this.

I almost pass Maybelle's but decide I want to talk to her before I pick up my delivery. I haven't seen her since everything went to shit. She called twice, and I ignored the calls each time because I just couldn't talk to someone else about what had happened. Hopefully, an in-person explanation will be a good apology.

The lunch rush is in full swing, so I park across the street. A blissful combination of freshly baked bread and cinnamon hits me as I walk through the door. I head upstairs to the cafe and spot Johnny chatting with a couple at one of the tables. He stops mid-sentence when he sees me and hurries over to wrap me in an unexpected hug.

"You had us worried, girlie," he says as I hug him back, slightly overwhelmed by the odor of cigarettes that always clings to him. He releases me and pats my arm, his eyes looking a little wet.

"Sorry, I would have come by sooner, but..." I shrug. "I hadn't even made it home before last night. Is Maybelle around?"

"She is, just head on back. She's in her office."

"Thanks, Johnny."

The loud chatter of the restaurant is replaced by the clank of plates being washed and the cooks shouting over each other as I pass through the door to the kitchen. I dodge a waitress carrying a full tray of food and weave my way back to the offices.

Maybelle's door is half-closed. I knock once as I push it open. She jumps and shoves something in her drawer.

"Sorry, is this a bad time?" I ask, hesitating in the doorway now.

"Don't be ridiculous," she says, coming around her desk with a big smile on her face that doesn't reach her eyes. She's wearing a bright red dress with a sea blue scarf and glittery black flats, but the dress is wrinkled and her hair is in a bun instead of its usual curly chaos. She doesn't have any makeup on either.

She gives me a brief, tight hug, then leans back and pats me on the cheek. "There's been a lot of rumors all over town about what happened in Rudie's. Everybody thought you were dead for a while. Someone was even saying the NWR had wiped out the entire clan."

"They definitely killed some of them. Some of the weres too," I say with a sigh. "We're lucky there weren't that many of the terrorists, or it would have been a massacre."

"Here, sit down," she says, herding me to a folding chair that sits facing her desk. She sits in another one across from me and smooths out her skirt. "Now, I know it's a bit trivial, but I thought it might cheer you up to hear they've already started construction on the apothecary. In a couple of days, you can go and see it if you want."

"Already?" I exclaim, sitting up straighter. "You move fast. I'm glad my ingredients just got delivered. I'll have to start brewing as soon as I can."

"Hopefully, the brewing can be a good distraction for you. I'm sure the next couple of months won't be easy," she says, patting my knee.

"No joke," I sigh. "A representative from the vampire council is coming to town at some unknown point to see me as well. We have no idea what they want."

"To see you?" Maybelle asks, her voice going hard.

"That's what Lydia was told," I say, confused at her sudden change in demeanor.

"You can't trust them, no matter what they tell you or offer you. Stay away from them if you can," Maybelle says through gritted teeth.

"I'll be careful, but aren't they on our side?" I ask taken aback. I've never seen Maybelle angry before, ever.

"No, they're on their own side. They'll do anything they can to gain power. Promise me, Olivia, promise me you won't trust whoever they send. You have to keep your guard up," she says, leaning forward and reaching out to grip my knee tightly.

"Okay, I promise," I say, patting her hand awkwardly.

She raises a brow like she doesn't believe me.

"I really will," I insist.

"All right," she says, shaking her head. "And I don't mean to rush you out, but I have some things I need to finish up on a deadline. Will I see you later this week?" she asks as she stands.

I stand as well, confused. "Um, sure."

"Stay safe, sweetie," she says, pulling me into a brief hug before shooing me out of her office and shutting the door.

I stand in the hallway, dazed by the whole interaction. She's never run me off like that. Why does the vampire council representative have her so flustered?

The expression on Maybelle's face bothers me all the way to the warehouse. I park across the street from

Gerard's warehouse and text Lydia for a quick up-date. I was already worried, but now I'm extra anx-ious about the visit.

I walk up to the door and realize I don't see the packages outside. Surely, the delivery driver wouldn't have left them inside. I grab the handle and find it's locked.

I frown and step back. I had left it unlocked when I was last here. I tilt my head to the side; I suppose Emilio could have locked it.

I knock loudly three times, wait three seconds, then knock one last time. I hear footsteps inside, and the door swings open, revealing a bleary-eyed but slightly cleaner than normal Gerard.

"You're back," I say dumbly.

"Obviously," he says, squinting at me, then opening the door wider. "It's there."

He points at a pile of boxes just inside the doorway set on a grungy looking pallet.

"Oh, great, thanks," I say, stepping inside and grabbing the first box. He nods and starts back to-ward his office.

"You could have told me it was the NWR in town," I blurt out. It's been bothering me since I fig-ured out who had taken Patrick.

Gerard stops but doesn't turn around to answer.

"I didn't know who it was," he rasps. "Just had a bad feeling, that was all."

There's no way. Absolutely *no way* Gerard is a Di-viner. I can't think what else he might be implying though.

I carry my boxes out to the car, and by the time I'm done, I'm starting to regret the flannel. It's not nearly cool enough outside to be carrying heavy stuff in the afternoon sun without working up a sweat.

19

I double check that I haven't missed anything inside.

"I'm all done!" I shout across the warehouse. Gerard waves a hand out of his office in acknowledgment.

I climb back into my car and lean my head against the steering wheel. Always more questions than answers. All I want is one calm day. That shouldn't be too much to ask.

My phone rings. It's Lydia.

"Hey," I answer as I start the car and pull out into the street.

"Before Javier wakes up, I just had to ask if Patrick was with you, or if we need to be concerned?" Lydia asks, her voice tired.

"He's with me, and he's fine. I wouldn't rule out being concerned though."

"I know you don't want to hear this, but—"

"Then don't say it," I interrupt.

"Olivia, he's not safe."

"I'll take my chances," I snap.

Lydia is quiet, and I take a deep breath and change the subject. It's too early to be fighting. "You hear anything else about when the council rep is supposed to show up?"

Lydia huffs, annoyed. "No, they don't tend to give much notice, but this is getting ridiculous."

"Figures. I'll talk to you later then."

"Be careful," Lydia says quietly.

I end the call and rub my fingers across my brow. I really can't blame Patrick for being angry with Javier. Things got messy and people got hurt and Patrick isn't thinking straight. Javier is also kind of an ass sometimes. I don't want to be caught in the middle though.

I stop for groceries on the way home. It's been a

while since I've had a home cooked meal, and a quick soup sounds great. It takes me less than ten minutes to get in and out, my passenger seat now full of bags.

I park my car in the usual spot in my driveway. The sunset almost fifteen minutes ago, so I know Patrick will be up. Part of me wants to just sit in the car and eat some of the ice cream I got before it melts instead of going inside to face Patrick and everything that has happened.

I sigh and open the door. The sound of shouting makes me freeze, one foot on the ground, halfway out of the car. There's more than one voice. I lean back in to grab my jacket and yank the glovebox open, grabbing the gun as well.

I run toward the house, trying to stay low and keep quiet. There's no sign of another car. The front door is still intact, but it isn't shut all the way. I step onto the porch cautiously, avoiding the creaky parts, and peek in the living room window. The blinds are down, but I can see two figures through the narrow slits. A man is standing over Patrick, whose lip is bleeding.

I stand and kick the door open in one fluid motion, my heart pounding out of my chest. I find the sight on the end of the gun and fire twice, the gunfire cracking loudly inside the house, but all I hit is the wall. The man has disappeared, and I never even saw him move.

I blink rapidly. Did I imagine him? I take a step back, scanning to see where he has vanished to. Patrick is yelling something, but I can't hear him over the ringing in my ears.

I back into a hard chest.

3

I freeze, but he doesn't move. His chest is cool and I can feel the magic that keeps him alive stirring under his skin. As if I needed any more proof he was a vampire.

"Quite the warm welcome, Ms. Carter. Both your pet and you attacked me without so much as a hello," he says in a lightly accented voice.

I swallow and step away from him, turning around very slowly with the gun lowered. He's at least six feet tall, with a sharp jawline and slightly hollowed cheeks that are softened by dimples. He's smiling, his fangs poking out over his full bottom lip. His thick, wavy auburn hair, which is smoothed back, sharply contrasts his crisp black suit. He's lean, but he's probably ripped under the suit.

"Who the fuck are you, and what are you doing in my house?" I say in measured tones. I should have called someone, or at least texted Lydia, before I walked in here.

"Reilly Walsh," he says, bowing with a flourish. "The representative sent by the esteemed vampire council to investigate the appearance of the NWR in a small, unimportant town in the middle of nowhere."

I edge toward Patrick, who is still sitting on the floor, glaring at Reilly.

Reilly smooths a hand over a wrinkle in his suit jacket and looks between us, raising a brow. "I believe you were told I was coming?"

"Sure, just not your name or when you'd be here or *why* you were coming," I say, finally tucking the gun in my waistband. It's useless against someone like Reilly. "Or that you'd be walking into my house without an invitation and attacking my friend."

Reilly scoffs. "He attacked me. I was well within my rights to kill him."

"Are you kidding me?" I exclaim, taking two large steps forward before Patrick pulls me back.

"Not worth it, Olivia," Patrick whispers into my ear. Normally, I'm the reasonable one and he's the hothead.

My skin is tingling, and I have to pull Novak's magic back sharply. How did he live like this? I seem to be on the verge of accidentally electrocuting someone every time I get mad.

"He has a right to be here; you don't. Get out. You can talk to me at the clanhouse, but you are not staying here."

"As a representative of the council, I have a right to go wherever I need to in the course of my investigation," he snarls, his dimples disappearing along with his smile.

"You are out of your jurisdiction, buddy," I snarl back. "I'm a witch. You don't get to tell me what to do. Now, get out."

"Make. Me," he says, baring his teeth after each word.

I have the same odds of winning the lottery as I

do of landing a hit before he kills me. I grind my teeth together, and Patrick tightens his grip on my arm; he obviously has no intention of letting me do anything moronic.

"This is stupid," I say, jerking at my arm until Patrick finally lets go. Reilly watches me, his brows pinched together. "I'm getting my groceries out of the car. If you hurt Patrick while I'm gone, I'll *find* a way to kill you."

I stomp back out the front door, slamming it uselessly behind me. My car door is still open. I slap it shut and walk around to the passenger side to get the bags. I hook them all on my uninjured arm, then turn around and walk into Reilly once again.

"Seriously?" I say, stumbling back against the car. "Personal space. It's a thing."

"You're the one that keeps walking into me. Perhaps try watching where you're going?" he says, those dimples making a reappearance. I want to kick him in the teeth.

"Did you come out here to help me carry in the groceries, or is there something you wanted?"

"I did want to talk, privately," he says as he hops onto the hood of my car and makes himself comfortable.

I set the bags back in the passenger seat and cross my arms. "Well? Get on with it."

"I thought southerners were known for their hospitality?" he pouts. "Maybe it's just this town."

I stare at him. He obviously just likes the sound of his own voice. He's hot, in a rich city boy kind of way with his slick suit and perfect hair. I'm sure girls normally fling themselves at his feet, panties already halfway down their legs. Hell, I would have been one of them if he hadn't come in and attacked Patrick.

"As I said before, I'm here to investigate the incident with the NWR, and most importantly, to make sure none of them are left."

"That's great," I say, though my tone says *I don't care.*

"I also intend to find Martinez, and in a show of good faith, the council is going to work with a witch in order to arrest him and bring him to trial. You were their choice. It'll make a good headline. Witch Gets Justice With Help of Vampire Council," he says, waving his hand through the air. "The journalists will come up with something catchy, I'm sure."

"Awesome, let me know when you find him, and I'll come kill him for you."

"We definitely need to catch him alive. The council was very insistent on that point."

"The council can go fuck themselves."

"Such bold words," Reilly says as he leans back on his hands. "Do you know Aaron Hall?"

"I know of him, why?" There's no way, just absolutely none, that they know what happened, but that doesn't stop my heart from doing a pitter-patter in my chest.

Reilly tilts his head to the side, looking me up and down in a way that should be flirtatious but instead leaves me feeling exposed.

"He's supposed to be a Finder, which would make things simpler. The coven should be trying to get some good PR, so I imagine they'll even lend him out for free."

Of course. He's a Finder. It makes sense for them to ask about him. This is fine.

"No one has any idea where Martinez is. It's not like a Finder can search the entire country for him, what's the point?"

"We'll have him search the local area first, just in

case. If we need him to search a larger area later, we'll do so."

"Sounds like you have a well thought out plan–"

"You're going to come with me when I talk to them."

I stare at him, mouth hanging open. "No, I'm not."

"What do you want, Olivia? More than anything?"

"For you to go away and never bother me again," I say, rolling my eyes.

"Not to find your mother?"

He says it so casually, as if it's a trivial matter. Something he can joke about. I clench my hand into a fist to keep the sudden heat of electricity from escaping.

"My mother is dead. Has been for years," I say with gritted teeth.

"Most likely," he agrees pleasantly, as though he can't tell I'm furious. "However, the medical records and death certificate Detective Brunson found were faked."

"What?" I don't want to go through this again. The sick hope already curling in my gut feels like a betrayal. Why is he trying so hard to get my help? As far as he should know, I'm not special.

"He knew that, didn't he tell you?" Reilly asks, tilting his head to the side. "Perhaps he didn't get a chance to before he died. Or perhaps he never intended to; you did get a bit obsessive about finding her when you were younger."

I don't respond. I can't.

"Come with me tomorrow evening to talk to the coven, and I'll tell you what I know about the faked records," Reilly says, hopping off the hood of my car.

"Why do you even want me there?"

"Because I am demanding, unreasonable, and secretive. I'll see you tomorrow just after sundown,"

Reilly says with a smile before disappearing without a sound.

I stand, stunned, and stare at the spot he just occupied. My mind is spinning as I think back to the day Brunson told me he had found her, and that she was dead. I had no doubt then that he was telling me the truth. Why would he lie about that? And despite what Reilly implied, I have a hard time believing he would. I hate everything about today.

I grab my bags out of the car and walk back inside. Patrick is sitting in the middle of the living room next to what used to be my coffee table. It looks like someone was slammed down on top of it. One of the legs is on the other side of the room.

"Are you hurt?" I ask, dropping the bags on the counter and fishing out my ice cream.

"No, but my pride may never recover," Patrick says as he stands. "I've never seen a vampire move that fast."

"I'm not convinced he isn't teleporting." I find a spoon and take a bite of ice cream.

Patrick stares at his hands, strangely quiet.

"Are you sure he didn't hurt you? Or threaten you?"

He hesitates just long enough to make me worry, then looks up with a smile. "He didn't, it's fine. Don't worry about me."

4

T he blinds are drawn tight, so the room is pitch black. I check my phone. It's only three-thirty in the afternoon. Just enough time to get started on some of the brews for the apothecary before the sun sets.

I groan and rub my eyes. I'm still tired, probably because of the nightmares that keep waking me up every few hours.

I roll out of bed and find my clothes. Mr. Muffins is waiting for her breakfast in the kitchen. She lets me pick her up for once, and I carry her around while I get her food together and refill her water. She's warm and soft and happily purring.

The coffee table, which was broken in Reilly and Patrick's fight last night, is still lying in the middle of the living room. I look at it, then just walk around it. That's a problem for another day.

The bandage on my arm has come half-loose. I pick it off and examine the wound. It's mostly healed. I press my hand on the wound and push the warm, healing magic into it.

It's always odd, healing myself. It turns into a

feedback loop almost. It's more tiring than healing anyone else, and harder to focus. I think the sensation and awareness of my body distracts me.

I exhale shakily and raise my hand. There's a light scar, but it's better than it was. I wad the bandage up and throw it away, feeling cleaner in a way, now that it's gone.

My workroom is still a wreck. That is actually a problem for today, so I crack my knuckles and choose a corner to tackle first. The door and windows open up first. I need the fresh air; it still smells vaguely of spice and smoke in here.

The bag that I carried everything in when I kidnapped Aaron is sitting by the door. I dump it out and start putting everything away. I pick up the flashlight, and the map catches my eyes. I reach for it slowly, my fingers tracing the back. She's dead. I know that. I shove it back in the bag and shove the bag in the corner.

One bag of trash, two sets of brewing instruments scrubbed, and a shiny stove, and I'm done. Now it's time to get everything dirty again.

I run through a mental list of the healing potions that might sell best. Headache potions, of course. Potions to keep bad dreams at bay and help someone sleep. I haven't made a Sweet Dreams brew in years.

My fingers trail over the cauldrons, as I think. I get to the cast iron cauldron and pause. The iron is rough under my fingers. It brings back memories I haven't thought about in a long time. When I was younger, my mom would sometimes just make a cider in the cauldron, then share it with the neighbors and tell them it was a good luck brew. They always walked away with a warm belly and their heads held a little higher. It's been a while since I've used this cauldron, and it feels neglected. It seems right to brew the Sweet Dreams potion in it while I'm full of these good memories.

I grunt as I pick it up. The cast iron cauldron is heavy and unwieldy, but the sturdiness is what makes it good for this brew. I light the fire underneath it and turn it down low. This is a potion to brew nice and slow. No rush, no stress.

I open the chest that I keep all my dried plants in and grab a bundle of lavender and the sweet alyssum I picked a couple of weeks ago. It still smells lovely even though the flowers have wilted.

The crystals are a different matter. I open the drawer and look over them, biting my lip as I consider each one. I need something cool and steady.

My hand drifts away from the usual crystals to the little pile of abalone shells in the back of the drawer. I smile as I wrap my fingers around one. The sound of the ocean is soothing, rhythmic, and relaxing. These will be perfect.

I fill the cauldron with water before it gets too hot, then put in a handful of chamomile tea in. The leaves begin a merry dance around the pot, forming swirls within swirls. Next is the lavender. The water deepens to purple as soon as the plant dips under the surface. It breaks apart quickly, and the little buds of lavender join the tea leaves in their hypnotic dance.

The alyssum I warm in my hands first, rolling it between my palms until the scent is bright and new again. The petals unfurl as they hit the water, the bruises disappearing and the wilted petals smoothing out.

I let the ingredients settle in the cauldron as I grab my mortar and pestle. The abalone shells grind up easily, crunching into a sparkling powder that looks like stardust.

I hum a lullaby under my breath; my mom used to

sing it to me before I decided I was too old to be tucked into bed. I can't remember all the words now, but they're not important. It's the feeling I need.

I pick up my wooden stirring rod and tap the edge of the cauldron. The petals all sink slowly to the bottom, disappearing in the purple liquid.

I grab a handful of the powdered abalone shells and hold my hand high over the cauldron. I tap the edge again, and the potion chimes, the sound ringing out around the room, as it turns to a milky dark blue.

Little starbursts of light burst out of my hand, igniting the abalone shell with magic as it falls from my hand, catching on some unseen flow of magic that sends it swirling around me. They hover like a cloud of stars, swaying slightly in an unseen breeze.

I dip the rod into the cauldron and stir, slow and steady. The little, twinkling stars begin to move in rhythm with the rod as though they are being pulled along on gossamer threads. Each stir brings a little more into the cauldron. They glint in the potion, dreamy and beautiful. I keep stirring, almost unaware of the passage of time. The light is the room is dimmed, and I feel calm and comforted.

With one last circle, the last of the abalone shell is pulled into the cauldron, and I feel my magic settle into the brew. I lift the rod out and step back with a contented sigh, a warm, floral scent drifting lazily from the cauldron. If only everything could be this simple.

The sun is setting, so it's just a matter of time before Reilly shows up. He had said he would be here promptly after sundown.

I hear Patrick moving around in the closet; he always twitches as he wakes up. I walk into my bedroom and sit on the end of the bed.

Patrick opens the closet door and stares at me, blinking blearily. He looks like his old self for a moment. He has slept over regularly in the past, never in my bed, always in the closet. It's always been an unspoken agreement that I've never thought too hard about. I care about him too much to fuck it up with sex, especially since, while he is attractive, we don't have that spark that always leads to me making dumb decisions.

"Did you sleep well?" I ask, smirking at him.

He rolls his eyes and runs a hand through his hair, trying to smooth out the weird bump on the left side.

"Fantastic, as always." His voice is rough, and he sounds grumpy.

"Reilly is going to be here any minute." I stand back up, unused to this sullen version of Patrick. "Do you need anything? I might be gone most of the night. Will you be going out?"

"I can take care of myself," he says, his hand twitching. "I didn't come here to have you babysit me."

"I'm not trying to babysit you. I'm just making sure my friend is okay," I say, lifting my hands.

"You're treating me like Javier did, like I'm sick or a child," he says, jaw tense and brows pulled tightly together.

"Sorry I asked," I snap, turning and walking out of the room.

Patrick follows me sullenly, then walks straight out the front door. I sit down at the table and put my head in my hands. I hope he doesn't do anything stupid.

I look back down at my phone, my thumb hovering over his name in my text messages. I don't really know what to say to him. I don't know what his problem is, but I don't want him to think I'm angry. I drop my phone back on the table without saying anything. Sometimes it's just better to leave people alone when they've turned into a grumpy asshole.

I'm supposed to have dinner with Lydia after this meeting with the coven. She has some kind of update from Timmons. I needed to go to the liquor store anyhow; I've been out of tequila for far too long. It's going to be a long night too. I'll be headed to the clanhouse after dinner for the checkup.

I stand up and stretch. I'm wearing a T-shirt that says *Resting Witch Face* and a pair of low rise jeans. It's completely inappropriate for everything I'm doing today, my own personal little rebellion.

Mr. Muffins meows loudly, and I turn around to see Reilly crouched down on the floor, engaged in some kind of staring contest with her. I wish she would bite him or something; instead, she purrs when he runs a hand down her back. Traitor.

Mr. Muffins rolls over onto her back and lets Reilly ruffle the fur of her belly.

"Stop petting my cat," I say, feeling further betrayed. "I want to get this over with."

Reilly smirks at me and buries his fingers even deeper in the fluff. She bites him, and he jerks his hand away with a hiss. I smirk; maybe not so much of a traitor after all.

"Even your cat is cranky," Reilly complains. He stands and adjusts his suit. He is dressed just as formally as last night, and I can't help staring. He makes a suit look good. He's even wearing a tie today. "You can drive. I'm sure you know your way to the coven's meeting hall."

"Sure." I grab my things, pulling my jacket on, and head outside without waiting to see if he follows.

He slips into the passenger seat as I am putting the car in drive and looks around with a wrinkled nose.

"It smells odd in here. You should really get your car cleaned."

"I should smear garlic all over the seats," I mutter.

Reilly chuckles at that and rolls down the passenger window. "How long have you lived in this town?"

"I'm sure you already know." I hate small talk on a good day. I have no desire to chat with this asshole.

"True, what I don't know is, why here? You stopped in quite a few towns before you settled down here."

"I got a job offer here. It was just kind of dumb luck, no point in leaving after that."

"You're referring to the contract you have with the local clan?"

"Yes."

Reilly rubs a hand thoughtfully on his chin. "What dumb luck led to you getting a job?"

"What is this? Twenty questions? I'm already helping you."

"Let's do a trade, then. You answer a question, then I do."

I tighten my grip on the steering. He just does not give up. "Fine, but I've already answered one question, so it's my turn to ask."

Reilly waves a hand magnanimously. "Go ahead."

"What did you fuck up to get sent on a low priority assignment in a middle-of-nowhere town like this?"

He doesn't react, which is annoying. I was sure that was it.

"Perhaps this assignment is more important than you realize," he says easily. "I don't make mistakes."

I roll my eyes.

"Now, answer my previous question."

I tap my fingers against the wheel before answering. "I had just gotten a job as a waitress at Maybelle's cafe in town, but it was only part-time, and I was having trouble finding a second job. This girl stumbles in one morning, starts eating breakfast, then passes out. I grabbed her and realized it was blood loss, then kept her alive until the ambulance got there. Turned out she had lied about how many people had fed from her, so the last vampire ended up taking too much. It got back to Javier, and he paid me for it, then offered me a job. So, like I said. Dumb luck. I just happened to be in the right place at the right time."

"Interesting."

I don't like the way he says it, like it really is interesting and now he knows something he shouldn't. A hedgewitch shouldn't be able to heal, but the magic is so weak, it's never aroused suspicion before.

"How long have you worked for the council?"

"Almost ten years, though it seems like far longer."

He doesn't follow up with another question, seemingly content to stare out the window for now. I stay tense as we drive through town. The coven lands are on the north side. It's almost fifty acres, with its own subdivision, as well as several large buildings, including an old church only coven members are permitted to attend.

The old mansion McGuinness lives in is in the center of their little town. Before you can get to that, however, you have to pass through the main gate. I can see it already. The black, wrought iron gate looms over the road, both a sign and a warning. I've never tested the enchantments, but I know there are many. The Ignatius Coven isn't weak even if they are in a remote area.

I come to a stop next to the guard's station and roll down my window.

"Do we have an appointment or what?" I ask as the guard approaches.

"No, I thought a surprise visit would be more fun," Reilly says with a dimpled smile.

The guard leans down to look through the window. "Name?"

"Olivia Carter," I say. Reilly stays silent.

"Do you have an appointment?"

"Nope, but ol' Dermot McGuinness is an old friend. I'm sure he'll want to see me," I say with a straight face.

The guard snorts, then points at Reilly. "What about you?"

"I'm just her security. John Smith if you need a name," he lies smoothly.

The guard steps back, talking to someone through his radio. They argue back and forth for a moment, then the guard waves the gate open. I pull through, surprised they're actually letting me inside.

"You know they're probably planning on killing me or something as soon as we get inside."

"We can only hope they try. I'd probably get a bonus for the PR from that alone," Reilly said, tapping a long finger against his chin. "I've heard McGuinness is a hothead."

"That's a serious understatement."

The main road runs right into the circular driveway in front of the mansion. The lawn is perfectly manicured, with a large fountain spurting water about ten feet in the air in the center of the driveway.

Two ornate pillars stand on each side of the door.

The wooden trim around the large double door is carved into two figures, one holding a bundle of herbs, the other with fire in one hand and a lightning bolt in the other. Aris and Izul, the witches that founded the original council a millennia ago.

I park right up front and step out of the car, feeling wonderfully underdressed. The big, wooden door opens when we're halfway there, and Baldy steps outside. He looks rather angry.

"Hey, old friend," I shout with a wave as we approach.

"You are not welcome here, Olivia Carter," he says in his deep voice. His skin is already tinged gray; it's like he doesn't trust me.

"So welcoming, as always," I say with a grin. I'm a little mad that this is fun. Reilly is going to be smug about it later, I just know it. "Where's McGuinness?"

"You will not be seeing McGuinness," Baldy replies, crossing his arms. "You have one chance to leave before we report you to the police for trespassing."

Reilly takes one step forward, and then simply walks past Baldy through the open door. The only evidence he didn't teleport is the rush of wind I feel as he moves. How is he this fast?

"What the fuck are you doing?" Baldy bellows, rushing after Reilly. I jog after them; I definitely want to see it if Reilly beats the shit out of him.

I step through the door as Baldy gets a hand around Reilly's arm. Reilly pivots and smacks him in the chest. Baldy wheezes and flies through the air, past me, and straight into the wall by the door. The sheetrock crumbles under the impact.

Baldy wrenches himself free, his skin now completely gray, and runs full speed back at Reilly. Impervs are impressively dense. Reilly sidesteps the reckless charge and winks at me. Baldy skids to a stop at the base of the staircase that dominates the room. He whips around, preparing to charge again. He is not a fast learner.

"Enough!"

At the top of the staircase is McGuinness, his face as red as ever, and Scarlett on his left. On his right is someone I don't recognize though. She's young but most likely at least eighteen. She has platinum blonde hair and looks like she weighs a hundred pounds soaking wet.

"McGuinness, how lovely to see you," Reilly says, spreading his arms wide as though he's expecting McGuinness to rush forward for a hug.

"Who the hell are you?" McGuinness growls.

"Reilly Walsh, the representative sent by the vampire council to investigate the activities of the terrorist group known as the New World Reformation in relation to the recent incident in your quaint little town."

McGuinness snorts. "That's been handled. The witch council is considering the case closed. Do the vampires have nothing better to do?"

"Case closed? How sloppy," Reilly says, shaking his head in disapproval. "The main conspirator escaped custody. Do the witches have no intention of tracking him down?"

"We'll leave that to JHAPI. What do you want?"

"Aaron Hall," Reilly says simply.

McGuinness laughs. "Then we're both out of luck. That little shit turned up after some kind of bender. Confused, barely able to remember his name."

Oops. Guess I brewed that memory potion a bit too strong. It's not like I could test it beforehand though.

"He hasn't been able to perform even the most

39

basic magic since. His family had me send him home to be examined."

"A witch losing their magic right before it's needed? How convenient," Reilly scoffs. "That's impossible, and we both know it."

"Perhaps you can ask Olivia how it happened?" McGuinness snaps. "She was seen talking to him the night he disappeared."

I snort. "So did he refuse to help me find the missing vampires because he had already lost his magic? Or is he just as much a prick as you are?"

I stare McGuinness down, but my heart is pounding. I'm sure Reilly can hear it. He's going to have questions later, especially since I didn't admit to knowing Aaron. I should never have come here. Reilly is more demon than vampire with his shitty bargains.

"We're done here. You can get out, or I'll have you removed," McGuinness growls, crossing his arms. Scarlett and the blonde girl step forward like eager guard dogs.

Water wraps around the blonde girl's arm like a snake. I twitch when I feel a drop of water hit my cheek.

Reilly steps in front of me, his shoulders hunch slightly, and his posture shifts into something far more menacing.

"Attacking a representative sent by the council violates every treaty we have, McGuinness. Are you sure you want to be *that* coven?" Reilly growls, all pretense of amiability now dropped.

"I am done entertaining the whims of the vampire council. See yourselves out."

McGuinness walks away, but Scarlett takes a step down the stairs. She is eager to fight, as always.

Reilly turns his back on them and offers me his arm. "Alas, a wasted trip."

I slip my arm through his, even though it pains me to take my eyes off the threats. "As usual."

5

I don't know why he hasn't asked me about meeting with Aaron yet. We're halfway back to town, and he's been acting like nothing is wrong.

"Is there somewhere I can drop you off?" I ask, uncomfortable with the silence. "I'm supposed to have dinner with someone."

"Who?"

"Lydia Holland."

"Ah, Javier Moreno's attorney. Is she a friend, or simply acting as your lawyer?"

"Both," I say, tapping my thumb on the steering wheel.

"I'll join you. I've heard she's a very interesting woman."

"You're not invited."

"Good thing I don't care," he says, flashing those dimples again. "If you'd like to explain why you didn't tell me you had met with Aaron Hall recently, I might be persuaded to reconsider."

I grit my teeth. "There's nothing to explain. The conversation was so unimportant that'd I'd forgotten all about it."

"You are a very bad liar."

"I don't know what you're talking about," I say as I gun it through a light that just turned yellow.

"Where are we having dinner?" Reilly asks.

I sigh. "What difference does it make? You can't eat."

"So hostile," Reilly pouts. "And I could eat something, it would just be disgusting."

I drive just past Maybelle's and park along the street. The main dinner crowd is already filtering out.

"How quaint," Reilly says as he steps out of the car. "Maybelle's Cafe. That's very southern. Do they have chicken fried steak and pies?"

I roll my eyes. "Do you ever shut up?"

He mimes locking his mouth shut and throwing away the key. I bite my tongue to keep from smiling, pivot on my heel, and walk toward the restaurant. He catches up to me almost immediately and even manages to open the door.

I hurry through the store and up the stairs to the cafe. The smell of food is making my mouth water.

Lydia is sitting in a booth in the corner, her nose buried in her phone. She's in a suit as usual, but her steel-gray hair is down and curled nicely. It does nothing to make her look less intimidating.

"He insisted on joining," I say as I plop into the chair across from Lydia.

She looks up, confused, until Reilly sits down next to me.

"Reilly Walsh, council representative," he says, extending his hand across the table. Lydia reacts much better to meeting him than I did and shakes his hand firmly, all trace of surprise gone from her face.

"Welcome to Pecan Grove, Mr. Walsh. How are you enjoying your stay so far?"

"It's been extremely pleasant." He inclines his head

with a smile. "Olivia has been kind enough to agree to assist me, as well as drive me around town this evening."

I look at him like he's crazy, and I'm starting to suspect he might actually be.

"Oh, has she?" Lydia says. She smiles at me broadly, but her arched brow says I'm going to get fussed at later. At least Lydia understands he's full of shit too.

"Yeah, it's been a riot." I cross my arms and look around for the waiter. I need food if I'm going to endure this.

He appears right next to the table as though I summoned him. His face is familiar.

"I'm Kevin, and I'll be your waiter this evening. Can I get you started with drinks?"

Ah, of course. He was my waiter the last time I ate here. With Martinez.

"Water, please," Lydia requests with a smile.

Kevin turns to me next, his pen ready.

"Coffee and the biggest chicken fried steak you have, lots of gravy. Also a basket of biscuits."

Kevin smiles as he jots the order down; he must remember me. "Would you like to go ahead and place your food order as well?" he asks, turning back to Lydia.

"Sure," Lydia says, scanning her menu. "The Cowboy Stew."

Kevin nods and takes her menu, then looks at Reilly.

"Nothing, thanks," Reilly says, smiling wide enough to show his fangs.

Kevin the-almost-unflappable pales slightly, takes the other menus, and walks away at a perfectly normal pace even if his shoulders are a bit stiff. Most humans don't think they're scared of vampires until they meet one. Witches and weres are easier to treat just like anyone else, but vampires creep people out.

"So," Reilly says, folding his hands under his chin. "A human lawyer working for vampires and representing a witch. Quite the collection of friends you have."

"I suppose," Lydia says, matching his posture. "What about you? The youngest vampire in your position, though young is an odd word to pin on you. Sired by one of the most powerful clans, and in fact, sired by the vampire most believe will succeed Claudius when he finally turns to dust. I imagine you have much more interesting friends."

Sired by the Sacrum Tenebris Clan leader? Seriously? There were three original vampire clans once paranormals started getting organized. Sacrum Tenebris, Familia de Sangre, and Ānjìng De Sǐwáng. They're all still in power today, in some way. Sacrum Tenebris and Familia de Sangre are two parts of the vampire council. The third is a newer clan that formed around the time Europeans began settling North America.

A cold chill runs down my spine. I've been threatening and being a huge pain in the ass, to someone way out of my league. This guy has the power to make me disappear. It wouldn't even be hard for him.

"You're not wrong." Reilly laughs, his dimple brightening his face and almost distracting from the hint of fangs under his lips. "Still, this town has certainly attracted all types."

"There's more room to do things a little differently out here, where we're unimportant," Lydia agrees with a nod. "That attracts the right sort of person."

"Very differently indeed. Moreno's clan is certainly a shining example of propriety. How long has it been since there was a death? Before the last week, of course."

Lydia's hand tightens around her silverware, still wrapped up in the little paper napkin. "A little over seven months."

I look at Lydia, a little confused. Only seven months? Javier had stressed that they took every care not to kill the neckers that came to them. Surely, they weren't just killing people left and right before I showed up. "It's lovely to see such a high survival rate among the new sires and the clan's resources. Moreno's methods are widely admired, well—by the people that matter at least," Reilly says, leaning back in his chair.

Resources. He says it like they aren't people. It'd be less insulting for him to call them neckers. And I can't imagine who wouldn't approve of what Javier has done. It's better for everyone.

"Olivia is coming to give the bi-weekly checkups tonight, actually. If you are interested in the process, I'm sure she can go over it with you," Lydia says, her hand still tight on the silverware.

"I needed to speak with Moreno, so the timing is perfect. I am very interested in the process."

Kevin appears with the basket of biscuits, and I eagerly grab one. I need something to do with my hands and mouth before I start asking questions that make me look stupid. Questions I obviously should have asked sooner. I was just so focused on the paycheck.

I shove half a biscuit in my mouth and chew, my cheek puffed out like a squirrel. Reilly looks at me with a grimace distorting his face. I glare at him and take another big bite.

"Timmons sent me an interesting email," Lydia says, turning to me.

I swallow uncomfortably. I should have asked for a water too. "Concerning Martinez?"

"Yep," Lydia said, making her lips pop on the 'p'. "Apparently, the NWR released a video featuring Martinez claiming they were attacked, unprovoked, for defending themselves against a marauding vampire."

I rub my hands over my face. "But there are no clues on where he is, are there?"

"Not yet, at least not any the JHAPI agents are willing to share with us," Lydia says, stealing a biscuit. "If they can narrow down the region, they'll be able to put a Finder on the case. No such luck yet."

Our food and drinks arrive together. The smell makes my mouth water. Kevin's hands only shake a little when he has to lean past Reilly to set my plate in front of me.

"Thanks, Kevin," I say with a smile.

"No problem. Need anything else?"

"I'll take a water," I say, already cutting into my chicken fried steak.

Kevin nods and hurries away. The table is quiet for the next minute or so as I shovel food in my mouth, Reilly watches with horrified fascination, and Lydia looks between us, her brows pinched slightly.

"I understand you intend to help with the investigation?" Lydia asks in-between bites.

"Somewhat. The council wants reassurance the NWR's influence is gone from the town. They are, of course, interested in locating Martinez as well."

My water arrives, and I gulp it down eagerly.

"Olivia has generously offered to assist with the investigation while I'm here and, if any leads on Martinez are found, lend a hand in apprehending him."

Lydia's eyes flick to mine. I shake my head slightly, and she lets it go, for now.

"The clan is willing to help as well. You have Javier's number?"

"I do."

I see Maybelle come up the stairs to the cafe. I catch her eye, and I'm about to wave when she sees Reilly. She freezes, her shoulders tensing. She immediately turns and walks back downstairs. I poke at the last bite of my chicken fried steak. Her hatred for him seems almost personal, though I have no idea how she would have met him before this.

"Can you slide out? I need to use the restroom," I say, poking Reilly's arm, then immediately remembering who he is. He doesn't seem to mind though and slides out of the booth before I have a chance to get unnecessarily nervous.

I slide out as well and start winding my way to the back of the restaurant. I do need to pee, and then I intend to track down Maybelle and see why she's acting so oddly.

I pass by a crowded table, bumping into a chair. I feel a hand on my arm and turn around to tell them to let go before I rip their fingers off, but my words die in my throat.

He's a spitting image of his father. Dark, almost black eyes. His hair is shaved short now, nothing like the long twists he had worn in college.

"Zachary," I swallow. "It's been a while."

"Four years," he says, his jaw clenching and unclenching. His hand is still tight on my arm. "Four years since the day my father died and the girl I called my sister disappeared without a trace. And that's all you have to say? It's been a while?"

I shrug, glancing around like I might be able to find a way to escape. My hands are clammy, and I feel like I might suffocate.

"How's Debra?" I ask like an idiot.

"Where did you go after you left? Back on the streets?" he demands, ignoring my question. His nostrils are flaring, and his teeth are bared like he wants to rip me apart. "Is that what you're doing here? Selling the drugs my dad tried to save you from?"

I rip my arm out of his grip, anger finally overtaking the guilt. "If you just came here to try to make me feel bad, you can fuck off. You never even wanted me there, or do you not remember that?"

"You were part of our family, and we needed you," he says, his voice raising loud enough to attract some odd looks.

"Did you somehow track me down just to come guilt trip me over leaving?" I ask.

Reilly is walking over to us. Fuck.

"No, but when you're name came up in a case connected to the NWR, I volunteered for the task force," he says, pulling his badge out of his pocket. It says JHAPI in bold letters at the top, with his picture underneath.

"Howard Z. Brunson," Reilly reads, leaning over Brunson's shoulder. "Our JHAPI liaison?"

Zachary whips around, startled, and takes in Reilly. "Who are you?"

"Reilly Walsh, council representative," he says, holding out his hand. "I believe we'll be working together at some point."

Zachary shakes his hand but looks like he couldn't care less who Reilly is. He turns back to me. "I've got some follow up questions for you, Olivia. Come to the station tomorrow morning around nine am," he says, immediately turning to walk away.

"No."

My answer stops him in his tracks. He turns back, a muscle in his jaw twitching. "Excuse me?"

"Everything I know is in my statement. I have

nothing to add. You can read that and watch the interview. I'm not talking to you," I say, crossing my arms.

"This is not optional," Zachary snaps.

"Am I under arrest?"

He glares.

"I'll take that as a no." I glare right back. He doesn't scare me; never has.

"I've found she responds much better to a delicate sort of bribery," Reilly says, leaning toward Zachary conspiratorially. "She seems to get a bit stubborn if you phrase it as an order. Issues with authority, I think."

"Shut the fuck up," I snap at Reilly. He's not helping.

"Always looking out for yourself first. I guess old habits die hard," Zachary says, his eyes clouded with something more than just anger. He turns and walks away. Half the restaurant is staring at us, the other half are whispering.

"What?" I challenge the room. Everyone is quick to avert their eyes. I stomp off to the bathroom. I need to pee even worse now.

6

"I must say, I couldn't really see the family resemblance," Reilly comments after five minutes of silence.

I don't respond.

Reilly sighs and shifts around like he's bored. "What exactly did you do to make him hate you so much?"

"I don't want to talk about it," I snap.

Zachary being here is like a slap in the face. I still remember that day like it was yesterday. He had answered the door without even checking to see who it was first.

Seeing the men in uniforms, their faces drawn and eyes red, was all either of us needed to understand what had happened. Debra had walked over from the kitchen, looking to see who it was when neither of us answered.

She had screamed. She had begged, and pleaded, for them to tell her it wasn't true. Zachary had simply crumpled. He sat by the door, face blank, staring at nothing.

And it was all my – no. I couldn't do this again. The past needed to stay in the past.

"How did you end up sired by some big wig vampire?" I ask, needing something to distract me.

Reilly looks at me from the corner of his eye. "A question for a question, remember?"

I grip the steering wheel a little tighter. "You're a real piece of work."

The rest of the drive passes in silence. Reilly's presence is like an itch under my skin. He's always pushing, needling.

I was able to warn Javier that he was coming to the clanhouse before we left the diner. I assume Lydia warned him as well. As I pull into the driveway, I wonder if that was the right choice.

What the fuck?

Javier is standing on the top step in a black suit with a wine colored shirt. Emilio is to his right in full, ridiculous Victorian regalia. The rest of the clan is spread out like a greeting committee, lined up according to their weird little hierarchy as best I can tell. There are odd gaps here and there, and I realize it's for the ones they lost recently. I'm not sure if they're making some kind of statement, or if it's just a ritual. Knowing Javier, it's probably somehow both.

Everyone is dressed well. They look polished, and the front of the house is practically sparkling. It's like they prepped for meeting the Queen or something.

I park in my usual spot and climb out of the car. Reilly follows suit and walks toward Javier without waiting for me to catch up. He's not moving at the insane speeds I've seen him use, but he's moving faster than any human could without sprinting. He makes it look effortless.

"Reilly Walsh, you are welcome here," Javier says with none of his usual flirtatiousness or flair. He bows low, and every single vampire follows suit.

"Your hospitality is accepted," Reilly says. Only then does everyone rise from the bow.

"Please join us inside. I can show you the house," Javier says. "Are you hungry?"

Everyone files in after Javier and Reilly, and I'm left standing in the driveway, forgotten. It's a relief. I was worried Reilly would follow me around like a parasite while I did the checkup.

I walk around to the side entrance I normally use and step inside. This area of the house used to be some kind of servants' quarters I think. There are a few small rooms, all used for storage now, down a long hallway that connects to the kitchen, and a staircase that leads upstairs.

I head upstairs to the usual room and knock once before walking in. All the neckers are already gathered here. Normally I see them more or less one at a time, but judging by the hunted looks on their faces, they're all hiding in here.

"Is everything okay?" I ask. Surely, it's not just Reilly's presence that has them so scared.

"Never been better," Leslie scoffs. She's a skinny brunette who's been here longer than I have. She hated me when I first started; I think she thought I had some special relationship with Javier and was all kinds of jealous. Luckily, she got over that real quick when she realized I wasn't interested. She was a practical sort of person.

"The council representative might come watch part of this, just so you know," I say as I walk over to the chair I always sit in.

The room isn't large. There are two high back chairs arranged in front of a fireplace that's never used and a bookshelf on the opposite wall filled with books in foreign languages. French, I think. There is one narrow window, but it's blacked out like most of the windows in the house. The only other decoration is a bland landscape painting hung above the fireplace.

I sit down, and Leslie takes the initiative to come sit across from me. I've developed a sort of ritual with them. It's intended to put them at ease as much as it is just practical.

Leslie extends her hands, and I meet her halfway, palm to palm. All my healing really requires is skin to skin contact. If it's bad, it's easiest for me to be touching the wound, or at least near it. For this, it doesn't really matter.

"Any dizziness, headaches, or nausea?" I ask as I prod at her with my magic, searching for wounds or blood loss. I heal a bruise on her back and scrape on her knee.

"Nah, I've been good, and taking those brews you gave us like clockwork," Leslie says, puffing out her chest in pride. She's something of a leader among the others, so I'm hoping they're all taking them now.

The constant feedings do put a strain on their bodies. The brews I gave them help with absorption of nutrients and ever so slightly increase the amount of blood their body can recover. If they weren't being fed on regularly, it would probably give them high blood pressure.

"Thanks, Leslie. You're all good," I say with a nod.

She gets up, and the next girl takes her place. More bruises, an unhealed bite mark, slight anemia. It's never bothered me before, but today I can't help wondering what they would be like without my healing. Would they be drawn and anemic? Would the vampires have already asked them to leave?

The next girl sits down. She's a young, pretty thing with dark brown hair and cheekbones that could cut glass. Her full lips and big eyes make her look like a doll. She smiles and holds out shaking hands. She has probably never been healed before.

"It's all right, it won't hurt at all. You'll just feel a little warm, maybe itchy if I heal something," I say, trying to be reassuring. Most humans still don't understand magic, and there is a lingering fear in some communities. People tend to either be fascinated by it or shun it along with those who possess it.

I press my palms to hers and almost flinch as my magic spreads through her. Her back is a mass of bruises, and there are claw marks on her arm I couldn't see under her cardigan. The back of her head is bruised too. She's lucky she doesn't have a concussion.

"What the fuck happened? Why didn't they send you to me?" I demand.

The girl glances back at Leslie before she answers.

"It's no big deal, we knew you were coming today. Javier didn't want to bother you," the girl stutters in a thick southern accent.

"Who hurt you? They shouldn't be losing control like this." I don't want any more vague answers today, this is ridiculous. They should be taking better care of themselves than this. Javier shouldn't have kept her from me.

"It—it doesn't matter. I'm fine, and you can heal me now, right?"

"Just tell me—"

"It was Patrick, all right?" Leslie interrupts. "Javier asked for a volunteer, she stepped up. She got hurt. We just didn't want to upset you. We know you two are friends or whatever."

I shut my eyes for a moment and take a deep breath. They're not really the ones I want to be yelling at. I'm going to have a very blunt conversation the next time I see Javier.

I heal her quickly, the magic leaves me in a rush, and I feel...fine. I should be more tired than this. It wasn't anything extreme, but my healing magic has always been weak and quickly depleted. I took barely any of the magic when I stole it. I refuse to worry about it now though; there's enough going on today already.

The door opens as the girl is standing, and Javier walks in, followed closely by Reilly.

"Olivia performs the checkups here," Javier explains, stepping to the side.

Reilly looks around the room, and at each of the neckers, before settling on me. "Please continue."

Leslie has to shoo the next person to me. It's a young man, another new arrival. He holds his hands out like the others, but they are shaking. I grasp them firmly and smile at him reassuringly.

I don't have to heal him at all. If he has been fed on, it was brief and healed up on its own. He's in perfect condition. I release his hands, and he hurries to the back of the room. Everyone stays still and quiet, waiting to see what the vampires want.

"Any of my clan's servitors would be happy to feed you," Javier says, gesturing broadly at the room.

I look at them, huddled in their groups, and disagree. A few look eager, but more of them look scared. Leslie is one of the eager ones, she's standing a little in front of the others. She's wearing a low cut black shirt that accentuates her best assets. Her blue eyes are taking in Reilly's clothes, his hair, and his easy confidence. I look away and swallow down something that feels like jealousy, which is ridiculous. I'm obviously still upset with the break up with Tyler and not thinking straight.

Reilly walks towards the group, taking his time and looking at each of them in turn. I wonder what he is looking for. A certain smell? Does he want them afraid? Is he looking for someone who will let him do more than feed?

He stops when he gets to Leslie. "What is your name?"

"Leslie," she purrs.

"May I feed from you?" he asks, holding out his hand.

She places her hand in his and nods.

"Please take him to the front room, Leslie," Javier instructs.

Leslie nods and leads him away, her hips sashaying and a proud smile on her face. My stomach twists uncomfortably. It's ridiculous, he's not going to hurt her, and it doesn't matter to me who he feeds from.

Javier clears his throat, and I tear my eyes away from the closed door. "Can I assume Patrick is staying with you?"

"Yes, and he's fine so far. Upset, but fine," I say with a shrug. It's really too bad I can't heal emotional damage.

"Come with me," Javier says, tugging on my elbow. The neckers begin whispering as soon as we step out of the room; I'm sure they have tons of new gossip to dissect.

Javier leads me through the house to his room and waves me inside.

"I wanted a little privacy. Reilly won't be able to hear us from this far away," he says as he closes the door behind us. He doesn't continue though; he simply walks to the window and sighs.

"Javier, out with it," I say, leaning back against the door and crossing my arms.

"You need to convince Patrick to come back here. It's not safe for him to be away from the clan, feeding without supervision. I don't want to have to force him to return," Javier says, his face blank and his posture relaxed.

"He hates you right now," I say quietly.

Javier's face falls, and his hands tighten into fists. "I know."

"He's really not in control?" I ask. I have to know for sure. "He seemed upset yesterday but not violent."

"It comes and goes. I thought the same, and I tried to let him feed from someone directly, but he –" Javier shakes his head. "He threw her across the room and then tried to kill her. I had to stop him, for his own sake, and I hurt him. I should have stopped him from leaving too."

Patrick had left that part out. Perhaps he really was still somewhat feral. A surge of hatred for the NWR, for Martinez, and for Chevy swelled up inside of me. They had no right to hurt any of us like this.

"I can try to talk to him, but he said he had left the clan. That's usually final."

A muscle in Javier's jaw twitches. "Until I accept his renunciation, it means nothing."

"All right." I don't know what to say or do. Javier is not quite what I'd call a friend, and I don't really care to sit around and talk about our feelings.

"So, is Reilly staying here, or can I leave?"

"He said he was staying with you," Javier says. "He also brushed off all my attempts to persuade him to stay here instead."

"He's such a pain in the ass," I grumble.

"Be careful of Reilly Walsh," Javier says, standing back up straight and pulling himself together. "I cannot protect you from him, no matter how fond I am of you or how much I value the work you do for me."

"Fond of me, are you?" I say with a smirk.

Javier winks. "Yes, terribly fond. You're my favorite witch."

I roll my eyes, but I don't really mind it.

"I'll see you again week after next. And just send them to me if they need healing next time," I say, opening the door. "I don't like it when you wait."

"As you wish," Javier says, joining me. He slings his arm around my shoulders as we walk down the hall. I elbow him in the ribs, and he removes the offending appendage.

"I wonder how long he's going to take," I say, glancing at the time on my phone. I want to check on Patrick; I don't like leaving him alone for this long. "Do you think he'd be offended if I just left?"

Javier frowns at me. "Perhaps, don't risk it."

"You're no fun when you're like this, Javier," I say. "I'm going to go wait in the kitchen."

Javier nods and heads over to a necker who has been trying to get his attention.

I head downstairs. Some of the vampires are milling around, whispering among themselves. Ada Talbott, a more senior vampire nods, in my direction, but the others all give me a wide berth. Patrick is the only one who ever attempted friendship. I'm not sure what the others think of me.

I'm not sure what I think of them either. Some of them take after Emilio with their lace and Victorian dress, others just look like the average person on the street. Only a few seem to have gone goth. They keep their fangs extended constantly, which honestly makes them look ridiculous.

I slip into the kitchen and look around. I'm not hungry after that big meal, but I could use a drink. I pull open the fridge and poke around. Water, boring. Lemonade, but that just doesn't sound good right now. Way in the back, I finally find a beer.

"Thank god," I mumble as I pull it out and pop the top off. It's cold and exactly what I needed. I take a long swallow, tilting my head back.

"You make it look delicious."

I cough and sputter, glaring at Reilly, standing across from me in the kitchen.

"That was fast."

"I was feeding, not fucking her," Reilly says, shrugging one shoulder.

I laugh despite myself and shake my head at him, which earns a smile.

"You are ridiculous," I say before taking another long drink. I guess I need to finish this quickly.

Reilly tilts his head. "I don't know that I've ever been described as ridiculous before."

I shrug and take another drink.

"Why aren't you staying at the clanhouse?" I ask, twirling the bottle in my fingers. It's been bothering me since Javier told me.

"I prefer to stay close to my assignment," Reilly says.

Close, right. I wonder if he pulled Leslie in close when he fed or if he just bit, sucked, and walked away.

"Right." I finish my beer and throw the bottle away. As soon as we get out of here, I'm questioning him on what he knows about my mother. I upheld my end of the bargain after all. "Do you need to do some formal goodbye, or can we just leave?"

He chuckles. "We can just leave."

Emilio is at the door like some kind of clairvoyant butler. He opens the door and bows deeply. Reilly doesn't acknowledge him as we walk outside.

Some of the tightness leaves my shoulders as we step out into the cool, night air. It's a relief to know the first visit is over. No one died. No one was horribly insulted.

It's pitch black outside. There's hardly even a moon right now, and the light from the town is just enough to make the stars seem dim. We climb in the car, and I turn it on, the headlights illuminating the front yard. I text Patrick we're headed back, partially to warn him Reilly is still with me, and partially just because I've been worried all evening and want to make sure he's still at my house.

That done, I drop my phone in my lap and pull out of the driveway. The road twists and turns, the trees looming over the road. Reilly is sitting in the passenger seat, alternating between staring at me and out the window.

"So, was your, uh, feeding good?" I ask to fill the silence. If he's going to stare at me, he can at least talk to me.

"It was satisfactory," he says, running a hand through his hair.

"That sounds like what someone says after they eat at restaurant they'll never eat at again," I say, raising a brow.

"Sounds about right." He smirks.

"Do people really taste that different?"

"Yes and no. Blood is blood, but some people taste more robust. I am spoiled in the capitol."

"I guess it makes sense that you'd get all the best neckers there."

"Of course," Reilly says. "It is strange though, the way they beg to be bitten. Most prey run from their predators."

"Can't say I really understand it either," I say, rubbing at my neck. Just the thought of it brings back unwelcome memories and makes me shudder. "I can see being curious, I guess, but the neckers always act like it's the best thing in the world."

"We can make it feel good," Reilly says, leaning toward me. "If you ever find yourself overwhelmed with curiosity, I'd be happy to help."

"Actually, the only thing I'm curious about is what you know about my mother's death," I say, gripping the steering wheel tighter. "I went to the coven with you, that was the deal."

"You waited longer to ask than I expected," Reilly says with a grin. "I thought you were going to ambush me as soon as we walked out of the coven's meeting hall."

"Well, I'm asking now." The whole fiasco at the coven had distracted me, and seeing Zachary again hadn't helped. Reilly doesn't need to know all that though.

"The death certificate was created by someone the council knows to be, let's just say, easily persuaded," Reilly says. "Two months before he died, Brunson requested an internal investigation. It was quickly determined that quite a few death certificates this person had created were faked. The only thing we don't know is who requested that he forge it, or why."

"Can you find out? Can I talk to this guy?"

Reilly doesn't respond. I glance at him, but he focused on staring out the window again.

"Reilly, I want to talk to him," I say with a frown. "I have a right to some answers. She could still be alive."

"You're being followed," Reilly says.

"What?" I check the rearview mirror automatically. There is a car behind me, but I have no idea how long it's been there, and it's fairly far back.

"Whoever it is followed you to the clanhouse, the

car was parked down the street. They picked back up as soon as you left."

"Is it NWR? Or someone from the coven?" I demand. "Did you see them?"

Reilly rolls his eyes. "Calm down, I don't think it's either. We can find out for sure though."

"How?"

Reilly turns to me with a shit-eating grin.

7

"Are there any roads you can turn down coming up?"

"Um, yeah," I say, trying to remember what roads connect to this one. I make this drive so often, I don't pay attention to the roads I don't take. "There are a couple."

"Turn down the next one, then pull off the road and shut the car off. We'll need to get into the tree line as quickly as we can."

The next road is right after a curve in the road. I take the turn sharply, drive over the bridge that runs over a dry creek, and pull off into the grass. There isn't much space between the road and the tree line, so part of the car is still on the narrow shoulder.

I shut the car off and jump out, following Reilly into the trees. He leads me about ten feet past the tree line, then crouches down behind a tree. I squat beside him and watch, my heart racing from the short run.

I see the headlights first; it seems like he stops once he sees my car sitting there. Finally, the car drives past, definitely driving slower than the speed limit, and stops just before the road curves again. It sits there, and whoever is inside doesn't make any moves to get out.

"He's trying to decide if you're still in the car, or if he can risk approaching," Reilly whispers, his lips way too close to my ear for comfort.

"I'm going to go see if I can tell who it is," I whisper back. The trees are thick, and unfortunately so is the underbrush. I pick my way through carefully, stepping over what I can to avoid thorns.

"I can just tell you who it is if you'd like," Reilly says as he follows me.

"If you already know who it is, why are we even doing this?"

"I wanted to make sure."

The car is plain, black, and completely average. It's the kind of car you drive when you're trying not to attract attention, or you're just cheap. I pause. It has government plates. So not the NWR. I get a little closer but still can't see through the tinted windows. Not that I need to. I know it's Zachary.

"It's your biggest fan," Reilly says.

"Why is he following me?" I ask, my nails biting into my palm.

"Based on what he said earlier, I imagine he's trying to catch you selling drugs."

I glare at Reilly. "I'm going to go tell him to fuck off."

Reilly grabs my arms, stopping me before I even get to take a step. "Not tonight. He's on the phone with someone, and he's about to leave."

"If he leaves, I can't kick his ass."

Reilly sighs, and I suspect rolls his eyes, but I can't see clearly enough to tell for sure. "Right now, you have leverage. You know he's following you, but he doesn't know you know. Try to be smart for once and use that your advantage."

"Being straightforward doesn't mean I'm being stupid," I say jerking my arm out of his grip. "Sometimes it's best just to confront people and get it over with."

"Have you ever tried another way?" Reilly asks, doubtful.

Zachary's car starts moving again. He turns around and drives back the way we came.

"Guess I have to now." I stomp back to the car, and Reilly follows.

I'm relieved to see Patrick on the couch when we walk in, but I pause in the kitchen. He's staring at his hands, and they're shaking.

"How could you go back there?" he asks, so quietly I almost can't hear him.

"I do the check-ups on the neckers every other week," I say, taking a cautious step forward. Reilly is standing quietly behind me. "It was a good thing I went too. One of them was pretty banged up."

Patrick's head snaps up.

"It wasn't my fault," he growls. "Is that what Javier said? He's lying!"

His eyes are bloodshot, and his fangs are extended. Fuck.

"Reilly, can you give us a minute? I want to talk to Patrick alone." I don't know what Reilly will do if Patrick attacks him again, and I don't want to find out.

"He's hungry," Reilly says, stepping closer instead of leaving. "How long has it been since you fed last, Patrick? Since you left Javier's?"

"Reilly, just go," I say, shooting him a glare.

Reilly hesitates, staring at me. "Why are you willing to risk your life just to help him?"

"Really not the time," I say, shoving at his chest. He moves this time and walks back to the door.

"If you kill her, I'll make sure you regret it," Reilly says to Patrick before stepping outside and slamming the door shut behind him.

Patrick is still focused on me, his breath coming in short pants.

"Patrick, Javier didn't tell me anything, I—"

"Liar!" he says, unfolding from the couch and taking three quick steps toward me. "I can smell him all over you. Did he finally get you in bed? I've never been sure why you haven't jumped into bed with him. You'll fuck anyone who looks at you twice. Did you let him feed from you too?"

My face heats, and I want to punch him in the mouth.

"What the fuck is your problem?" I demand, trying to keep from shouting, and failing.

Patrick's hands curl into fists, and he tenses.

"If Javier fed from you, I should be able to," he hisses. He takes another step forward, and his movements are jerky, like he's fighting with himself. I grab a vial of holy water from my jacket pocket and curl my fingers around it. I should have been more prepared for this.

"You're not in control, Patrick, this isn't you."

"No." He laughs, the sound high-pitched and grating. "No, this is me. It's always inside of me, Livvy; you just don't like to see it. You want the jokes and the fun at bars, but I'm always hungry.

He takes another step forward, eyes locking on my neck. "I'll only take a little."

It's a testament to just how malnourished he is that I can dodge the first strike. He rushes at me. I flick the stopper out of the vial and sling the holy water at him. It splashes the arm he holds up to block it, some of it hitting his neck and face. He growls as it burns but lashes out and grabs my arm before I can get another potion out.

Instead of pulling me to him, he shoves. I hit the wall, my head bouncing off the sheetrock, and crowds in close. I shove my free arm in his throat, holding him back, just barely. He's stronger than me; I can't do this forever.

"Patrick!" My voice breaks. "Stop it. You have to stop!"

He's leaning in closer, and my arm is collapsing slowly. I shove again with all my might, and his eyes finally snap up to mine.

He freezes. His hand trembles, and he stops pushing quite so hard on me.

"Livvy," he sobs. "I'm so hungry."

"Let me help you, please," I whisper. "Let me take you back –"

"No!" he shouts, moving away from me so fast, I almost fall forward. "No. I won't go back."

He runs out the front door, leaving it standing open behind him. I run after him, my legs shaking. I almost trip on the porch when Reilly steps into my path.

"Let him go," Reilly says, wrapping an arm around my waist and pulling me flush against his chest.

"No," I struggle against Reilly's grip, but I can't get his arm to budge. "He's going to hurt himself, or someone else. He can't. I can't let him."

"I can stop him."

Reilly finally lets go, and I turn around so I can see his face. "But let me guess, you want something in return?"

"Always," Reilly says without a hint of humor on

his face. "Tell me what you were really doing with Aaron Hall the night he disappeared."

I stare at him. I can't lie outright; he'd know. I wonder how close I can get to the truth without betraying secrets that would make my life forfeit. I don't have time to bargain either. Patrick needs to be stopped now.

"I kidnapped him," I say, biting the inside of my cheek nervously. "Drugged him at the strip club and took him to the warehouse and forced him to find Patrick for me. I guess the memory potion fucked his magic up, I don't know. I've never exactly tested it on someone."

He searches my face, looking for some hint of deception.

"Reilly, please," I beg.

"I'll be back tomorrow after sunset," Reilly says before disappearing. I stand on the porch for a moment, feeling lost. I can't see or hear either of them now. I have to hope Reilly keeps up his end of the bargain and doesn't hurt Patrick.

It finally registers that I'm shivering from the cold. I turn and walk back inside, my energy drained, new bruises forming on my arm.

I wish Zachary was here so I could kick his ass and work out some of this pent-up frustration. Having him in town and hearing all this stuff about my mother brings back all the memories of late nights pouring over missing person reports and Jane Does found all across the country. Women with amnesia. Dead bodies, unclaimed.

Brunson and Zachary had been with me through the whole thing. Zachary was the one who had let me grip his hand until it bruised when Brunson told me my mother was dead. Had Brunson known then? Or had he thought he was telling me the truth? If the death certificate had been faked, it could be because someone wanted us to stop searching.

I pause in the living room and realize how big of a mess the house still is. I won't clean it up anytime soon though. My mom would have fussed at me until I cleaned it up if she was here. If she was alive.

I grab the coffee table leg and throw it across the room with an angry shout, then stand there panting. I don't know what I'm waiting for. I should have done this as soon as Reilly told me the records had been faked. I can't help Patrick tonight, but I can do something. I have to know for sure if she's dead or alive.

I rip open the junk drawer in the kitchen and dig until I find it. A map of the entire United States. My hands shake as I unfold it. Partly from hope. Partly from fear.

It's reckless to use a map that covers the entire country. Even the best Finders need a smaller area to search. Aaron Hall was weak, and that means I am too. But I don't care. I have no idea what happens if the person you're looking for is dead either. The Finders never talk about it.

I spread it out on the floor and smooth a hand over the wrinkles until it lays flat. I close my eyes and take a deep breath, searching for the subtle and warm Finding magic. It's there, almost hiding from the electric magic I took from Novak. I pull on it and let it take over.

I stretch my hands out over the map, and the magic moves under my skin, a warm trickle. It spills from my fingertips, and the map shudders and lifts. The certainty I felt as I searched last time isn't there. I don't know if the map is too big or if it simply can't find the dead.

Bright lines of red slip down from my hands like

puppet strings and slide across the map, searching and searching. The tendrils crinkle the paper of the map as they slide across it.

The magic grows hot. One of the red lines burns a hole through the map. Then the next and the next. It surges down into the floor, and I try to jerk away and end the magic, but I can't. The magic has crept up my arms and is holding on to me now. I can't stop.

I fall. Light flashes around me. Then absolute darkness. I can feel my arms burning where the magic is curling around them, but I can't move. I can't scream. I can't see.

Memories of my mother come rushing back to me. Her face. Her laugh. The first time we brewed together. Her eyes and mouth wide as she screams the first time I stole her magic. When I didn't know what I was doing. A dusty room with candles all around. Blood and gray ash all around me.

Olivia. Olivia. Olivia. Olivia.

The pleading.

The day she left.

Burning arms. The smell of smoke filling my nose.

8

I wake up all at once, my breath coming in great, heaving gasps. My vision is blurry. I rub my hand over my eyes and hiss in pain.

My hands are covered in stripes of blisters that swirl all the way up my arms. I sit up, shaking, and look around. The map is ash on the floor, and there are scorch marks all around me.

"Shit," I whisper hoarsely. My throat is raw, as though I've been screaming. I struggle to my feet and try to think. I have a salve for burns. It's in the work-room. I'm exhausted, and so is my magic. There's no way I'll be able to heal myself right now.

I stumble down the hall and through the open door to the workroom. I'm able to nudge the door to the mini fridge open with my foot, but I'm going to have to open the salve with my hands.

I grit my teeth, grab it and twist the lid open as quickly as I can. A blister pops, and my eyes water. I hate the feeling of burns; nothing hurts quite like it.

With shaking fingers, I spread the salve over my hands first. It itches like crazy as the magic seeps into my skin and begins to heal from the inside out. I have to take a break after my hands are covered. I slide down the wall and lean my head against the cool door of the fridge.

I knew she was dead. It was stupid to let Reilly rekindle that hope. I should probably stop all of this right now. Stop looking for a cover-up. Stop looking for her killer. Even thinking it makes me feel like a failure. She would have done anything for me, but I don't have her strength. I fell apart when she disappeared, and every choice I've made since then only seems to lead me farther down the wrong path. Brunson tried to help me, but after he died too, I just ran. I've been barely hanging on ever since.

I turn my hands over and examine the backs. The burns are fading, but the salve can only do so much, and I apparently can't heal this with magic. Red welts wind around each finger and the back of my hands. They reach up my arms, almost to my shoulders. I spread more of the salve over my arms. I have to pause every few seconds, panting against the pain.

Mr. Muffins pads into the room, stopping just inside the doorway.

"Come to judge me?" I ask in a whisper.

She swishes her tail behind her.

"I know, it wasn't my best decision."

It takes effort, but I stand and toss the half-empty tub of salve onto the counter. I need two things today; Zachary to stop stalking me, and apple pie.

I find my phone, and I'm relieved it's not even noon yet. It means I got hardly any sleep, not that passing out from misusing magic really qualifies as sleep. But it also means I have at least seven hours before I have to deal with a single fucking vampire again.

My hand twitches, still trying to heal, and I flex it uncomfortably. I can't walk around with these welts showing. Wearing gloves would raise even more questions than the welts themselves. I hurry back into the workroom. I have a cosmetic salve meant to cover pimples and dark circles under your eyes. If I put on enough, I might be able to hide the marks on my hands.

I rummage through a box meant for Maybelle's and find a small case of them at the bottom. I open it and scoop some out, rubbing it on like lotion. I breathe a sigh of relief when I see that it hides them. Mostly. It's good enough.

It'll only last for about eight hours, so I take the tub with me. I can't have them reappearing and have no way to cover them back up if I don't make it home again in the next eight hours.

I grab a long sleeve shirt out of my closet and pull it on. I'm not going to bother trying to use the cosmetic salve on my arms.

I catch a glimpse of myself in the mirror and decide to put some on my face too. I look like shit. The dark circles under my eyes fade away, along with the bruise on my chin I hadn't even felt until I saw it. There's not much I can do for my hair except put it up in a ponytail.

I pause in the kitchen, my hand on my jacket, then go the cabinet and grab the whiskey out of the cabinet. I unscrew the lid and take a long, deep swallow. I'm tempted just to stay here and finish the bottle. I slam it back in the cabinet. That'll have to be enough to dull the frustration for now.

Now, to deal with Zachary. The pie can be my reward.

The police station is quiet when I walk in. A woman in a uniform sitting at the reception desk looks up when I walk in. She seems to recognize me. I walk up, tugging my sleeves down, just in case a mark is peeking out.

"I need to talk to Special Agent Brunson," I say.

"You're Olivia Carter, right? That witch that got caught up in that NWR business?"

"Yes."

Chief Timmons comes down the hall, a stack of files tucked under his arm.

"Oh, Olivia, I wasn't expecting you today," Timmons says, approaching with a smile on his face. He shakes my hand firmly.

"I'm actually here to see Agent Brunson. We're old friends," I say with a smile.

"He hadn't mentioned that," Timmons says, his brows pinching together.

I shrug. "He's fairly private. Probably just didn't think it was pertinent."

"Ah, understandable. Let me show you to his office. He and his partner have taken over one of our conference rooms for the task force," Timmons says, pointing down the hallway to my right. It's in an area of the police station I haven't seen yet. "I'll walk you there."

"Thanks," I say, the fake smile still plastered to my face. The linoleum floor is dingy, and our shoes squeak with every step until the flooring changes to carpet at a fork in the hallway. We go right, but halfway down the hall Timmons pauses.

"I didn't want to bring it up when you were here last," he says, talking in hushed tones. "But Novak's funeral will be in two days. I'll be sending the details to Lydia. It will be in the morning, so unfortunately, the clan won't be able to attend, but I did want to give you the option."

I'm not sure if it's worse to go to the funeral of a

man you killed or avoid it. I swallow and clear my throat, trying to find my voice.

"I'll be there," I say finally.

Timmons pats my shoulder, then continues down the hall at a faster pace. I jog after him.

"By the way, any updates on the search for Martinez?"

"Not yet," he says. "The NWR has always been effective at hiding their members. We did search the entire tunnel. It led to the middle of the woods, but we can't find their trail after that at all. They treated the area with something that makes the tracking dogs lose their minds. The werewolves won't go near it either."

I shake my head. No one can ever accuse the NWR of doing a half-assed job of things.

The hallway opens up into an open area with six desks arranged in pairs. Each desk faces another in a line down the center of the room.

The conference room isn't hard to find either. There is a large window in the wall that provides a clear view of the room. Zachary is standing at the head of the table next to a woman with long black hair and eyes that look blue even from here. There's a whiteboard behind them with pictures of faces I recognize and notes under each. Martinez, before half of his face was melted off. Chevy. Even Novak.

The woman nudges Zachary as we approach. He stops talking and turns to see who is coming. His jaw tenses as soon as he spots me.

"Brunson, Ms. Carter requested to see you," Timmons says, poking his head into the conference room.

Zachary looks at me, barely keeping his face blank. I cross my arm and stare him down. We can talk in there in front of everyone, but he won't like it.

He says something quiet to the woman, then steps out of the conference room.

"Thank you, Chief Timmons," he says.

"Let me know if you need anything else, Olivia," the Chief says, patting me on the shoulder as he walks away.

Zachary and I stare at each other in middle of the room.

"What do you want?" he asks, crossing his arms to match my posture.

"Just wanted to chat. See if you found anything interesting last night on your little surveillance run."

He scoffs but brushes past me, taking the hint that this should be a private conversation. I follow him down the hall to an office. He opens the door, and I brush past him. He slams it shut behind us.

"I have a right to investigate everyone connected to the attack. Especially anyone who has a questionable history."

"Oh please," I snap, whirling around to face him. "You just want an excuse to give me shit. Quit trying to make this anything other than you just trying to get some kind of pointless revenge."

"You are so selfish," he says, shoving his finger in my face. "My dad believed in you. He said you wanted to help people, but he was wrong."

"I am helping people!" I say, slapping his hand away. "I'm doing good here, but you don't know any of that because you came here with your mind already made up."

"You abandoned us!" he shouts, a red flush darkening his face further. "You could have saved my mom, but you were gone and I couldn't find you!"

I take a step back, my heart dropping into my stomach. "What are you talking about?"

"Brain tumor. She lived for barely two months after we found out."

The room tilts, and I can't breathe. I had just assumed that if I left, they could just be okay. Debra had always been full of smiles and eager to feed you. She was ageless. I can't imagine her dead. I don't want to.

I try to walk past Zachary; I don't want to be here anymore, but he grabs my arm. His fingers dig into my skin right over a welt, and pain shoots through my arm. I stop and don't try to pull away, but I stare at the floor as I speak.

"I couldn't have saved her Zack." My voice wavers. I have a lump in my throat I can barely talk around. "My healing, it's weak. I can't touch things like cancer or tumors. I wouldn't have been able to— I'm sorry."

I pull my arm away, and his hand drops to his side. I open the door and leave him standing in the office, staring straight ahead.

9

I sit in my car, hot tears rolling down my cheeks. My arms are aching again, but I can't bring myself to care.

My mom is dead. Brunson is dead. Debra is dead. Patrick is basically feral. And then there's Reilly. The devil incarnate who will no doubt find a way to get me to sell him my soul.

I bash my hand against the steering wheel and shake it like it's the source of all my problems. I hate this. All of it. Life shouldn't be like this, just one tragedy after another.

Still grinding my teeth in frustration, I turn the car on and shift into gear. I'm going to get pie and a bottle of tequila, then go home and drink until I can't remember my name, much less how shitty my life is.

It's still the lunch rush at Maybelle's, so I have to park three blocks away. I wipe away any evidence I've been crying like a little bitch from underneath my eyes, then get out of the car and hurry down the sidewalk.

Maybelle's is crowded as usual, but the line at the counter isn't very long. An old man with a long white beard bumps into my shoulder as he hurries past me.

He mumbles an apology, then hurries out of the store. I don't even have the energy to glare at him.

I get behind the last person and check my phone. The only message is from Lydia, and it's informing me she has no updates. I shove it back in my pocket and wait impatiently for the line to move.

It takes less than five minutes, but it feels like longer than that.

"One apple pie, please," I say before the girl at the counter has a chance to ask what I'd like.

"Whole pie?" she confirms, fingers hovering above the register.

"Yep."

"That'll be twenty-five dollars," she says, holding out her hand for my payment. I grab the money out of my wallet and pass it to her.

She puts the money in the register, then walks back to the pie warmer and takes one out. It smells amazing. She sets it in one of Maybelle's pretty fall colored boxes, and then in a bag so it's easier to carry.

"Here you go," she says, passing it across the counter.

"Thanks."

I turn around and almost walk into Georgia.

"Olivia," she says, smiling warmly. "I was hoping to find you here."

"I guess I come here too much," I say with a half-hearted chuckle.

"It has become predictable," she agrees. I'm not sure if she's making a joke or not, so I simply nod.

"I understand that you heal the people the vampires feed on, I have a similar request."

"All right, is someone hurt?" I ask.

"Yes, since the fight with the NWR. We had hoped he would on his own, but there must be silver deep in his wounds we cannot smell. I do not think he will recover without help. Will you heal him? I can pay you whatever is necessary. Name your price."

"I'll do it. And you don't need to pay me; we can just call it a thank you for helping with the fight in the first place," I say, jumping at the chance to help. This is someone I can actually save. If I was in my right mind, I'd just take the money, but I can't. I don't want Zachary to be right about me.

Georgia looks surprised but nods. "All right. I have to run one more errand. Can I meet you back here in twenty minutes? I'll drive you out to the house."

"Sure, sounds good." I wanted to check out the apothecary anyhow. "Here, let me give you my cell number just in case."

She hands over her phone, and I type in my contact information.

"Thank you, Olivia. I will text you as soon as I am done." She walks briskly out of the store.

I grab a plastic fork, then back out. The apothecary is only a few stores down. I reach down into the bag and open the lid to the container the pie is on. It'd be a crime not to eat some while it's still warm.

The first bite is almost orgasmic. The crust is just flaky enough. The apples inside are soft and covered in just the right amount of cinnamony, sugary filling. I hurriedly scoop another bite into my mouth.

For all my skill in brewing, I can't cook anything this good. Debra had tried to teach me and laughed when my pie crust was dry and crumbly. I drop the fork in the bag and smash the lid down on the pie.

I hadn't lied when I told Zachary I wouldn't have been able to save her. Perhaps someone could have, but there's no way they could have afforded it. The waiting lists for those healers are also years long, just like organ transplants. Part of me is relieved I didn't have to watch her die, but I'd rather have had a chance to say goodbye. My fingers tighten on the bag. Who am I kidding? I had the chance; I was just too afraid to go back and face them.

The large coming soon sign hanging from the front of the apothecary distracts me from my thoughts. The storefront is with thick glass, and 'Maybelle's Apothecary' is etched into the glass in large, looping letters.

I cross the street and peer in the window. It's still empty inside. It looks like the contractors are still putting up sheetrock and building out the back. I still can't believe this is happening. It's something my mother had dreamed of. She wanted to open a little shop with just the two of us, and she was working on getting her guild membership approved before she disappeared. My hands and arms still ache, a physical reminder of the pain of missing her that I'll never be rid of.

My phone buzzes, and I turn away with a sigh. It's a text from Georgia. I'm looking forward to a distraction. Maybe they can eat this stupid pie for me too.

I don't hear anything, not a shout, or even the explosion itself. I'm flying through the air, and I can't see. I hit the ground and slide, asphalt scraping my cheek and chest.

There's smoke. I blink. Sirens. Blink. Someone is shaking me. Blink. Brown eyes and dark hair and a pale hand reaching for me. Blink. Georgia's face over mine. Blink. Blood in my mouth.

10

I gasp awake, reaching for someone who isn't there. It's dark in my room and dark outside. Javier is leaning over me, his wrist bleeding sluggishly. I can still see my mother's face like an aura in my vision. It's like I looked at the light for too long, and now it's all I can see.

I blink, trying to dispel it. The blood in my mouth distracts me, and I reach for Javier's wrist. I want *more*. I need it.

"Olivia," a sharp voice shocks me into full consciousness. There is an IV strung from my wrist to a pole next to the hospital bed. Fuck. I'm in a hospital.

"What happened?" I croak, wiping my mouth on the back of my hand. It leaves a smear of blood, and I have to fist my hands in the sheets to keep from reaching for him again. He tastes even better than I remember.

"The apothecary was bombed. You were caught in the blast," Javier explains. His face is downcast. I think he feels sorry for me. I'm furious.

"Was it the NWR? Is Martinez back? Do the police have any leads?" I bite out each question, my hands twisting further in the sheets. My entire body aches, and if my face looks how it feels, then it looks like someone tried to scrape half of it off. It would hurt worse if Javier hadn't shared some of his blood. It's an odd thing, the way it helps to heal. It can't really save anyone's life, but if you're a witch, the magic gives you a boost that helps your body heal itself. Most people find it disgusting and not strangely addicting like I do though. My jaw aches for another taste.

"They're assuming it's the NWR, but they have no idea who set the bomb," Javier says.

"Fucking fantastic," I say, shooing Javier out of the way and swinging my legs over the side of the bed. I bat away Javier's hands and yank out the IVs. "Is Georgia okay? I think she was there…it's all fuzzy."

"She found you after the explosion. She's fine," he says, trying to push me back down. "Olivia, they want to keep you overnight."

"No," I snap. "I'm fine. I'll go home and take a couple of potions. I can't pay this hospital bill anyhow."

Javier steps back, his hands held up in surrender. "Come to the clanhouse, at least. It'll be safer for you there."

The door opens, and Patrick steps inside, his eyes wide as he takes in the hospital bed and the IV. The wince he makes when he looks at my face confirms it's about as bad as it feels.

He walks toward me slowly, glancing briefly at Javier but ignoring him for now.

"You look like shit," Patrick says, a smirk on his face that fills me with relief.

"That's what happens when someone tries to blow you up, I guess," I say, grinning at him even though it hurts my cheek.

Neither of us is the type for apologies. Not the

traditional kind, at least. I know he means he's sorry, and he knows he's forgiven.

"Let me guess, you're trying to escape the hospital already?" he asks, walking around to the side of my bed opposite Javier.

"You guess right," I say. "Where are my pants?"

Javier crosses his arms. "You can have them when you agree to come to the clanhouse."

"I just want to go home! I need to feed my cat."

"It's not safe," Javier insists,

"Is anywhere safe?" I ask, throwing my hands in the air. "I was in a public place in the middle of the day, and someone set off a fucking bomb."

Javier opens his mouth to retort, but Patrick holds up his hand, stopping him.

"Javier, give us a minute?" Patrick asks.

Javier stares at Patrick over my shoulder, breathing hard, then nods and walks out of the room, slamming the door behind him.

Patrick waits a moment, shifting uncomfortably on his feet. "I'll go back if you go back."

I bite the inside of my cheek. He must be serious if he's actually helping Javier get me back to the clanhouse. It's a sharp change from the night before. I briefly wonder if Reilly is somehow coercing him to do this the same way he got me to go to the coven to look for Aaron Hall. Instantly, I feel guilty for doubting his intentions, but it could actually be the case knowing Reilly.

"If they're setting bombs, I'm not necessarily safer there," I say with a sigh. He's already won the argument, and he knows it.

"Then we might as well die together," Patrick says lightly, grabbing my jeans out of a bag sitting by the window and tossing them at my face. I catch them and roll my eyes.

My legs are shaky as I crawl out of the bed. I need a few of the potions I normally reserve for emergencies with the neckers. I yank my pants on underneath the hospital gown, then drop it on the bed and reach my hand back for a shirt.

"What the fuck happened to your arms?"

I snatch my hand back, trying to hide the welts even though it's too late for that.

"It's nothing, don't worry about it," I say quickly. "Just give me a shirt."

"Those look new. Did someone hurt you?"

I give up on modesty and turn around, hands on my hips. "No one hurt me. Just give me the damn shirt."

"Your boobs aren't going to make me forget my question. What the fuck did you do, Livvy?"

I bite my tongue to keep from yelling at him. I can't explain this without risking both our lives and everything I've worked to build here. My mother had made me swear to never tell anyone, not for any reason. It's the only promise to her I haven't broken yet.

"It was a brewing accident," I lie. "It's embarrassing and doesn't matter, and I don't want to talk about it."

I thrust out my hand again, barely stopping myself from stomping my foot too. Patrick glares at me but hands the shirt over. I slip both arms into the shirt.

There's a perfunctory knock on the door, then Reilly walks in, followed by Georgia and Javier. Reilly's eyebrows shoot up as I hurry to pull the shirt the rest of the way on.

Javier looks between me and Patrick, a muscle twitching in his jaw. Georgia brushes past them both, completely unconcerned. I finish buttoning the shirt before I look at them again.

"I seem to have arrived five minutes too late," Reilly says as he plops down in the only remaining chair. "What did I miss?"

I roll my eyes. "Glad to see you're all right, Georgia."

"I am glad to see the same. I was concerned you were dead when I first saw you," Georgia says matter of factly. "You were twitching."

"That's disturbing," I say, raising a brow. "How is your wolf? I can still heal him tonight if I need to."

Georgia frowns. "You don't look like you're in any shape to heal."

I shrug. "My magic is fine. You said he was getting worse and no good will come from waiting."

"If you are sure," Olivia agrees. Her fingers loosen their grip on the arms of the chair, like she's relieved. "I'll have him brought to your house."

This is why she's my favorite. She doesn't argue or baby me.

"Bring him to the clanhouse, actually," I say.

Javier breathes an audible sigh of relief behind me. I'm not sure what Reilly is thinking, but he doesn't look upset. I would thank him for whatever he did to help Patrick, but considering he took advantage of the situation to try to extort information from me, he can go fuck himself.

"The doctors aren't going to like you leaving like this," Javier says, already hovering. This is why he's my second least favorite. Reilly still holds the title of first.

"They can just try and stop me."

Reilly chuckles, and Javier glares at him. I guess Javier got over the formality from when they first met.

"Who even called all of you?" I ask

"I did," Georgia said. "I didn't know of any family, but I had Lydia's number."

"Lydia is harassing Chief Timmons for answers currently," Javier says, answering my question before I ask it.

"Has anyone heard from Maybelle?" I ask, suddenly worried. It didn't look like anyone was there when I stopped by, but...

"Lydia said she was at the police station," Javier says.

"Does someone have my keys?" I ask, patting at my pockets.

Patrick winces. "About that."

11

The phone rings and goes to voicemail once again. I sigh and drop my phone in my lap. I was hoping to talk to Maybelle tonight. I'm not sure when I'll make it into town again.

I slouch down in the back seat of Javier's sleek black car, arms crossed, and glare out the window. Reilly is on his way to the police station, and I'm relieved to be rid of him for a little while at least, but I wish I was there with him. I want answers.

"I still can't believe my car is totaled," I mutter.

"The car wasn't that great," Patrick offers.

"It was paid off!" I throw my hands up in the air, exasperated.

"You can use one of mine until you can afford a replacement," Javier says from the front seat.

"Not the point," I grumble as we pull into the driveway. My car is gone, and so is my chance at making a decent living. Maybe I can guilt Javier into giving me a raise. I think I've earned it.

Javier drives past the house to the garage and parks in an open slot. It's practically a parking lot back here, with all of the cars for the vampires and the neckers. Only Javier's cars are in the garage itself though.

Javier's phone rings as we get out of the car, and he hurries into the house. Patrick and I follow. He's tense as we walk in, his nose twitching as he looks around.

There's a vampire, whose name I've forgotten, downstairs. He stares wide-eyed at Patrick, then scurries off. Most likely to share the latest gossip with the other clan members.

Having Patrick back at the clanhouse makes everything feel right. He slings an arm around my shoulders as we walk into the kitchen, his fingers tight. I pat his hand comfortingly. It's always awkward to come back after a dramatic exit.

Georgia won't be here for a little while, and I'm hungry. My chest is starting to ache again, and my cheek is still swollen. I need food. Or a drink.

Patrick hops up on the counter, and I open the door to the freezer and dig out some ice. I wrap it up in a towel and hold it to my cheek.

"You think they have any tequila hidden in here?" I ask, opening a couple of cabinets.

Emilio appears in the doorway. "We do not, but some can be acquired."

"You never get me tequila when I ask for it," Patrick says with a fake pout.

"You have returned," Emilio says. I can't tell if he's pleased by this or not.

Patrick leans forward with a smile. "Did you miss me?"

"No," Emilio frowns, turning a glare on Patrick before looking back at me. "Olivia, Javier instructed me to go to your house and bring you whatever you require. What do you need?"

"You need to bring Mr. Muffins here. I'm not

leaving her alone at the house for a week if people are trying to kill me. So, you'll have to grab her food and her kitty litter. Don't forget the canned food in the fridge either, or she'll murder us all in our sleep."

Emilio nods, taking my requests as seriously as I would expect.

"I need all of my medicinal brews. My cauldrons too," I pause. The apothecary has been destroyed. I don't actually need to brew anything anytime soon. "Just the brews will be good, actually. I guess I'll need a week's worth of clothes too."

"I'll have it within the hour," Emilio says with a short bow before turning and striding away.

"Don't forget bras and panties!" I shout after him.

Patrick snorts.

"Not to kill the mood or anything, but you seem a lot...better today," I say, shifting the ice around on my cheek.

Patrick looks at the floor.

"Reilly fed me," he says quietly.

"You mean he found you someone to feed on?" I ask, confused.

"He did find someone for me to feed on after, but no," Patrick says, shaking his head. "He gave me some of his blood. It's something a stronger vampire can do to help someone regain control, but most won't because it weakens them."

"Javier gave me his blood after the attack, and in the hospital today. He seems fine."

"It's different," Patrick shrugs, his eyes downcast like he's ashamed of what happened. "To bring someone back from the verge of losing control, they have to give a lot more than what you took. Javier wanted to do the same for me before I left, but I wouldn't let him. He isn't powerful enough; it would have half-killed him."

"I've never heard of that before."

"It's not something that's widely talked about," Patrick says, sliding down off the countertop. "Someone just drove up. It's probably Georgia."

I dump the ice out in the sink and head to the front of the house.

Leslie is already at the door, and she opens it and waves the guests inside. Georgia strides in followed by a tall, bearded man. With his shaggy black hair, he looks like he should shift into a bear and not a wolf. He's holding another were, a shirtless boy with black hair who doesn't even look eighteen. I wonder if it's his son. The kid's face is contorted in pain, and his skin is covered with a sheen of sweat.

Georgia looks around, apparently never having been here before. Javier appears at the top of the stairs.

"Leslie, you may take them to the front parlor," he says as he walks downstairs.

She nods and leads the way to the same room I saw Javier laid out in less than a week ago.

"You can just lay him down here." I point to the floor in front of the couch.

The man lays him down, and I'm able to see the wound on his side clearly. It's not very big. It looks like someone stabbed him. Black tendrils are creeping from the edges of the wound toward his heart. I haven't seen a silver-infected wound on a werewolf in person before, but the signs are obvious.

"I appreciate your hospitality, Javier," Georgia says.

Javier nods graciously and stands out of the way near the door. He leaves a few feet of space between him and Patrick.

When I spoke with Georgia before, she hadn't seemed all that worried, but she's standing with her hands in tight fists at her side, and a muscle in her jaw is twitching. Perhaps the werewolf has gotten worse since we last spoke.

"I'll do what I can, but this might be worse than what I can fix," I say, laying my hands on the boy's trembling chest. His eyes are wide, and he looks terrified.

My magic stutters slightly, and for a moment I think I must have damaged it when I tried to find my mom. I take a deep breath, and it smooths out. I can feel the boy's heart, beating fast and hard from a mixture of fear and pain. There are no bruises or cuts other than the unhealed wound.

He feels warmer than a human would, but I think that must be because he's a werewolf. The flecks of silver in the wound are cold spots. I move my hand over it, and the boy jerks. I frown; this shouldn't hurt.

With little jerks, the silver slowly begins to separate and slither out of him. He twitches, and the bearded man presses his shoulders down to hold him still. The silver begins sliding out of the wound and winding up my hands. It makes my skin itch, but that's better than what it was doing to him.

Slowly, I feel the cold spots disappear. The wound still feels odd, like it has gone stale. I press my hand down over the wound as hard as I can, and the boy groans.

"Hold still, David, it's almost over," Georgia says in soothing tones. She crouches down by his head and smooths her hand over his forehead.

I should be tired now. Exhausted, even, but I'm not. It's like the pool of my magic has somehow gotten deeper. It doesn't take a genius to figure out how, though I had no idea stealing different kinds of magic would help like this.

Patrick and Javier have seen me heal before.

They've seen me exhausted from pushing past my limits, Javier especially, but I can't leave David like this if I can finish healing him. I push a little farther and feel blood finally begin to seep into the wound. The blood is dripping out onto the carpet now, and it seems to be flushing the wound clean. My jaws ache with something like hunger. I swallow and try to ignore the feeling. This isn't normal. The boy lets out a sigh like he's finally no longer in pain and stops trembling.

With every remnant of the silver gone, my magic is able to knit his flesh together from the inside out. The wound closes and smooths into a red, teardrop-shaped scar.

I move away carefully, and the silver falls from my hands to the carpet. My palms are slick with blood. Patrick is staring at me, brows knit together. "David, how do you feel?" Georgia asks, brushing a stray piece of hair back.

"I'm sorry, Mom," David says, his words slurred. "Didn't mean to be trouble."

I look up, my mouth hanging open. I had no idea she had a son, much less that he was the one hurt.

"He wasn't supposed to be there. He followed us and joined the fight against my wishes." Georgia smiles at me, tight-lipped. "His father, my mate, was killed a couple of years ago while traveling on pack business. The police investigated, but the NWR is good at what they do and good at disappearing their members when they need to. David could not stand to pass up the chance at revenge."

Georgia chuckles, but it is a humorless sound. "I can't blame him; he is his mother's son, after all."

"I'm so sorry, that's awful," I say, a quiet rage settling in my chest. The NWR has hurt so many people, and all for something so pointless.

"Thank you for healing him. I could not have stood losing them both."

I nod. "He still needs to take it easy for a while. There was a lot of silver still in the wound."

"I will make sure he rests," Georgia says as she scoops her son up. The bearded man squeezes Georgia's shoulder briefly, then nods in my direction.

"If he's still like this tomorrow, let me know. He should be back to normal after he sleeps though."

"I will," Georgia says. "He smells right now though. I am no longer worried."

Leslie walks Georgia, and the other werewolves back out. A tense silence settles over the room, and I have the urge to flee and let Patrick and Javier hash out whatever issues they're having.

"Olivia, Emilio, put your things in the room across from Patrick's." Javier pushes off the wall.

"Great," I say, standing up and holding my hands out in front of me so I don't smear the blood on anything else. "Is there an attached bathroom?"

"Yes," Javier says.

"All right, I'm going to go clean up," I say as I hurry out of the room. Neither of them moves to follow. I'm almost to the stairs when Reilly walks in the front door.

"Have you been murdering people without me, Olivia?" Reilly asks, nose twitching. He cocks his head to the side. "Is that from a werewolf?"

"Yeah, one of them still had some silver in him from the fight with the NWR. I healed him; it got a little messy." I hurry upstairs, hopeful Reilly won't follow.

I pause at the door to my room, and Reilly reaches around from behind me to open the door. I jump, then glare at him. So much for him not following me.

"You're welcome," he says, raising a brow and his mouth cocking up into a one-sided smile.

"I'm not thanking you for being creepy," I say as I walk inside.

The room is laid out exactly like Patrick's, though the walls are bare and the bed has a sedate, navy comforter set instead of the colorful one Patrick uses.

I head straight for the bathroom and begin scrubbing at my hands. The blood is already drying and starting to flake. It's under my fingernails too, and that's always a pain to get out.

"There was another bomb," Reilly says as he leans against the door to the bathroom. "It was at the cafe. An employee found the old bag it was in and thought it was odd. They tossed it in the dumpster behind the building, and that dampened the explosion enough that it hardly did any damage."

I stare at Reilly's reflection in the bathroom mirror and swallow uncomfortably. This could have been so much worse. The cafe had been so crowded that day, just like every other day.

"Why would the NWR go after Maybelle like that?"

"Why indeed?" Reilly asks. "That was Special Agent Brunson's first question as well."

"Didn't the NWR already take credit for it?"

Reilly nods.

"They'd take credit for someone they didn't like stepping on a Lego though," he says, shrugging one shoulder and waving his hand dismissively.

"Who would want Maybelle hurt like that? Everyone in this town loves her," I say, turning the water off and facing Reilly.

"Maybelle told the police there was no one who

would want to. That she couldn't think of a single person," Reilly says. "She was lying."

"She wouldn't do that," I say sharply. Maybelle has never lied in the time I've known her. She's always been ruthlessly optimistic and cheerful; it's my favorite thing about her.

"And yet, she did," Reilly says, spreading his hands wide.

"How do you know?" I demand, stepping toward him.

"I heard her heartbeat."

I roll my eyes. "Polygraphs are unreliable, and so is your hearing, apparently."

"Go ask her yourself. Perhaps she'll tell you the truth," Reilly says, stepping toward me so he can tower over me.

"She told me not to trust you," I say, pointing an accusing finger at him.

His lips close around the tip of my finger, and I'm too startled to jerk away, even as his tongue flicks across the tip of it, sending a spike of pleasure through me. My lips open slightly, and my breath catches in my throat. He pulls back, his cheeks dimpling in amusement.

"You missed a spot."

I lower my hand, a blush creeping up my neck. "Don't do that."

"Can you think of a good reason Maybelle would warn you not to trust me when she hasn't even met me?" Reilly asks, licking his lips slowly.

"You're with the council, and everyone knows you're power hungry, interfering assholes. There's a reason no one wants to catch the attention of the council."

He walks forward, pushing me back until I'm pressed against the bathroom sink.

"Maybelle is lying, and you need to find out why."

"I'll find out, but it's going to prove she's telling the truth," I say, jutting out my chin stubbornly. He might have distracted me with his little finger sucking stunt, but I'm not that easy to convince. My finger is still tingling though.

"I'd keep chatting, but that has made me hungry," he says with a wink before stepping away and walking back through the bedroom.

I step into the hall with a retort on the tip of my tongue, when I see Emilio with a very angry Mr. Muffins in a cat carrier. Emilio's sleeve is torn and his hair mussed. I've never seen it mussed before.

"Take your cat," he says, thrusting the crate into my hands. "I suspect it is possessed."

He goes into my room with the other bag, a couple of the neckers trail behind him, carrying the rest of my things.

I follow but can't help a glance back. Reilly is waiting at the end of the hall. He winks and smiles at me, cheeks dimpled and not looking nearly guilty enough.

"I do not have enough potions to deal with this," I whisper under my breath as I hurry into my room.

I lean in and inspect my face in the mirror. Thanks to the potions I took before bed, and the healing I did on myself, the bruising and scrapes on my face are mostly gone. The shower washed away the last of the concealing potion on my hands. The welts are still red and tender.

Emilio brought all my medicinal potions to my room last night. I grab the salve and work it into my hands and up my arms. The welts don't fade at all. I'm starting to worry they're going to scar. Perhaps because they were made by magic, they won't heal like a regular burn. I need to try to brew a stronger version of this salve, or maybe something new.

I press my palm to a welt near my elbow and prod it with my healing magic, then yelp as it shocks me. My palm is unmarked, but it feels warm and achy. I won't try that again anytime soon. I really need to figure out what I've done to myself, and soon.

There's a knock on my door.

"Just a minute!" I shout as I hurry back to the bathroom to pull on my clothes. I'm still sticky from the shower, but I can't let anyone see these welts. It's bad enough Patrick saw them.

Clothes finally on, I hurry to the door and crack it. Lydia is standing in the hallway in a crisp black suit, her hair pulled up into a chignon. I pull the door completely open and step aside to let her in. Mr. Muffins runs out as she walks inside. I hope she pees on Reilly's pillow or something.

"I'm glad you're up," Lydia says briskly. "Special Agents Brunson and Hawking will be here soon to take your statement."

"I don't have to go to the police station this time?" I ask as I walk back to the bathroom to finish getting ready.

"No, I insisted they come to you this time," Lydia says. She tugs the comforter straight, then perches on the end of the bed since there is nowhere else to sit.

"Are they still assuming the NWR is behind this?" I ask as I brush a little mascara on my eyelashes. It makes me look a little more awake.

"Yes and no." Lydia walks over to stand in the doorway. "Did Reilly tell you about the second bomb?"

I nod and turn to face her, leaning against the bathroom counter as I braid my hair.

"They have to investigate the possibility the NWR is, in fact, responsible. But the second bomb they found is making the agents question that."

"Reilly said Maybelle is lying about not knowing who might want to hurt her." I roll my eyes, still irritated about that.

"Did he say why?" Lydia asks, forehead furrowed. "She seemed adamant about finding out who had planted the bombs. She insisted the police provide extra security at the cafe as well."

"Apparently, her heartbeat gave her away," I scoff. "I think he's full of shit."

"It is strange though, for her to be the target," Lydia says thoughtfully. "She has to be hiding something. There's no way she wouldn't realize it if someone hated her enough to set bombs at two of her businesses."

"You'd think," I agree with a sigh. I don't want Reilly to be right. "I'm going to try to call her again."

"All right," Lydia says, looking at her watch. "Make it quick, I think they're already here."

I grab my cell off the dresser and dial Maybelle's number. The phone rings and rings and goes to voicemail again. I end the call and shrug, but I'm getting concerned. It's not like her to ignore me like this. A small part of me is just hurt that she hasn't checked in on me at all. I did almost die.

"Voicemail again."

"After the funeral, I can drive you into town to see her in person. I'm sure she's just caught up with the fallout, probably dealing with insurance," Lydia offers.

"Probably," I agree, shoving my phone in my pocket. "Let's go get this over with."

The house is strangely quiet, with all the vampires, and most of the neckers, asleep. Zachary's voice drifts upstairs, then Leslie's. It seems like she takes over Emilio's job during the day.

I follow Lydia down the stairs. Zachary and his partner are waiting in the foyer. Hawking looks up first, her nose twitching. Zachary doesn't look at me.

"Sorry to keep you two waiting," Lydia says, holding out her hand to Hawking first, then to Zachary.

"No problem at all. Leslie here promised us sandwiches for our troubles," Hawking says with a wide smile, hands on her hips.

She's wearing the usual JHAPI uniform, black slacks and jacket over a white button-down shirt. Her belt buckle draws my eye though. I stare for a moment before it makes sense. It's a pineapple turned sideways. What an odd choice.

"We can sit in the dining room, then." Lydia leads the way. I wave Zachary and Hawking ahead of me and trail after them. Zachary's shoulders are tense as he glances back at me. I look at him impassively even though my stomach is twisting and palms are sweating.

Lydia sits at the head of the table. Hawking takes the chair to her right, and Zachary sits down next to her so I'm forced to walk behind Lydia to sit on the other side of the table.

"All right," Hawking says, pulling out a notepad and a recorder. "Go ahead and start at the beginning when you got into town."

She looks at me expectantly. I take a deep breath and think back to that afternoon.

"I got some pie at Maybelle's, spoke to Georgia. She wanted me to heal one of her people," I say, crossing my arms and leaning back in the chair.

"Georgia?" Hawking asks. "She is the Alpha of the local werewolf pack, correct?"

"Yes."

Hawking motions for me to continue.

"I agreed to heal her packmate, but she still had a couple of errands to run, so I decided to go check on the progress of the apothecary. I don't really remember what happened next," I say with a shrug. "I just remember smoke and sirens, and then I woke up in the hospital."

Hawking nods, biting the end of her pen. "Did you see anyone you didn't recognize at Maybelle's Cafe? Anyone acting nervous?"

"No, but I wasn't really paying attention." I shrug.

"Has anyone sent you threats?"

"Not that I know of. I'm fairly certain Martinez wants me dead, but that's not exactly new information."

She scratches down a few notes. Zachary hasn't said a word since we got in here. He has his notepad out as well, but he hasn't written anything down. He has been glaring at me for the past five minutes though.

Hawking glances at him too and narrows her eyes at him. "Brunson, do you have any other questions?"

"No, I don't."

"All right," she says, tapping her pen against the table once. "I guess we're done, then."

She pushes her chair back and stands. Zachary follows suit.

"I had a question before you leave, actually," I say, standing as well. "Do either of you think this was the NWR?"

"We can't discuss an ongoing—" Zachary begins.

"No," Hawking interrupts. Zachary turns his glare

on her, but she ignores him. "I don't, and I intend to find out who is actually behind it."

"Any leads on who it is?" I ask, leaning forward. I'm glad Hawking is willing to talk to me, at least.

"Nothing solid. There's a suspicious person on the security camera, a man with a long white beard. Maybelle Williams is cooperating but somehow being completely useless as well. You know her personally, right?"

"Yes." I nod.

"If you can, get her to be honest with us. We can't help her if she's hiding things from us," Hawking says, tapping her pen against her leg, agitated.

"I'll do what I can," I say, disquiet stirring in my gut. Everyone is saying the same thing, and Maybelle isn't acting like herself.

Hawking nods. "We'll be in touch."

Lydia and I follow them out of the room. Brunson pauses just outside of the doorway. Hawking gives him an odd look, then rolls her eyes and continues on. Lydia follows her.

Brunson grabs my elbow as I go to walk past him as well. "Can I have a word?"

Lydia and Hawking are deep in conversation now, so I nod and lead him to the front living room. I let him shut the door behind us and plop down in one of the chairs.

"Why is there blood on the carpet?" he asks, staring at the spot where David had been lying the day before.

"Vampires." I shrug. Brunson looks between me and the spot, clearly concerned, then shakes his head and leans back against the wall.

"Did you ask me to talk so you could just stare at me?" I ask. I don't want to sit in here with him longer than I have to, and he doesn't seem willing to start whatever conversation it is he wants to have.

Zachary rubs both hands over his face, then finally looks at me. "Why did you leave?"

I bite the inside of my cheek. Why can't he just hate me and avoid me like a normal person?

"Does it even matter? I left. You hate me. Debra probably hated me. It's done."

He groans in frustration. "Maybe I just want to know! You owe me that much."

I lean forward, elbows on my knees and press the palms of my hands into my eyes. "Your dad promised to help me find my mom. He did that, and then he—"

I bite off the word, unsure of how to continue. The paranoia that followed and the worry over the way his tone with me had changed after he had found the information are hard to explain.

"He changed. You didn't see it, but he did. He avoided talking about my mother's disappearance, and her death, after he found her. He got angry with me when I said I wanted to find out who had killed her, said I needed to let it go. Which was the opposite of what he said when he took me in. I saw fear in his eyes, Zachary," I say, a lump forming in my throat. "Then those cops came to the door, and he was dead. I just assumed it was connected. It wasn't logical, and I didn't wait to find out the truth. I couldn't face either of you while I thought I was somehow responsible for his death."

"It wasn't—"

"I know," I interrupt. "Six months after he died, I got drunk and worked up the courage to look at the cause of death. A drunk driver hit him when he stopped to help someone change their tire."

I remember the pictures of Debra and Zachary standing by his casket, overwrought with grief. The

lines of men in uniform. The deep, wrenching realization of how much I had failed them. I'm tired, and
I want Zachary to leave, but instead he walks over to
the chair across from me and sits down.

"A stupid, pointless accident killed the best man
I've ever known. And I abandoned his family because
I was selfish and self-obsessed. Because I couldn't
watch you grieve while I was still grieving myself," I
say, my voice cracking on the end.

My lower lip trembles, and I dig my nails into my
palm to distract myself. I refuse to cry. Again. I stand
abruptly. This will have to be enough for whatever
closure Zachary wants.

"I don't know if I can forgive you," Zachary says,
eyes tired, face locked in a frown.

"Good," I say firmly. "Don't."

I walk out of the room before he can reply.

12

It's three a.m., and I can't sleep. The funeral is in five hours, and I'm going to look like the undead. I rub the heel of my hand across my eyes. Every time I try to go back to sleep, all I can see is my mother's face. I didn't even have this problem right after she disappeared. I can also hear the vampires in the hallway, whispering and laughing about whatever it is they gossip about. Between all that and dread for the funeral tomorrow, well today, sleep has been elusive.

Mr. Muffins is currently kneading my stomach, her claws pricking through the blankets. I sit up, dislodging her, and pick her up as I slide out of bed.

"How about we both go get a snack?" I ask.

Mr. Muffins meows and licks my arm. I take it as an affirmative. I'm wearing an old, worn T-shirt and baggy sleep pants with tacos all over them; hopefully, I can avoid running into too many people on my way to the kitchen.

I open my door and check the hallway, but it's empty. I pull the bedroom door shut behind me and readjust Mr. Muffins, smoothing down her fur.

I'm halfway down the hall when I hear a disgustingly flirtatious squeal from the room I'm about to pass, and I can't help myself. I edge toward the door and peek inside. I shouldn't have.

Reilly is with a different girl tonight, a redhead with long, straight hair. She's perched on his lap with her head thrown back in laughter and her arms wrapped around his neck. She whispers something to him as he trails a finger up the side of her neck. I should look away, but a sick curiosity keeps my eyes glued to the spectacle in front of me.

He smooths a hand across her cheek, and she quiets, her head tilting to the side with a breathy moan. She has got to be faking it; no one is that excited before anything is even happening. He leans in slowly, flicking out his fangs at the last moment. They sink in slowly, and she sighs like it feels good, her back arching. Reilly's eyes slip shut as he sucks. I swallow, my throat suddenly dry. Warmth pools in my stomach, and I'm not sure if I'm jealous of the girl, or if I want to be the one sucking her dry. I can almost taste Javier's blood in my mouth. It had made me so *hungry*.

Mr. Muffins meows loudly, clearly ready for her snack, and Reilly's eyes open. He doesn't stop feeding, and I'm frozen to the spot, watching him watching me. He pulls away slightly, licking the puncture points as his arms tighten around the girl and she moans. I finally find my feet and hurry away.

"You are such a bitch," I mutter to Mr. Muffins as I jog down the stairs. Reilly is guaranteed to give me shit for that. I am such an idiot.

A girl I've seen around the house often passes me on the stairs, her eyes flicking between my pants and sleep-rumpled hair. I frown at her, but she doesn't comment.

Thankfully, the kitchen is empty. Then again, it's

almost always empty. I don't think the neckers cook very often.

I drop Mr. Muffins on the floor and dig through the cabinets for a bowl. All the dishes are slightly fancy, but I guess Mr. Muffins does deserve the best.

I grab a white and gold china bowl and set it on the ground as Mr. Muffins winds between my legs, purring like a lawnmower.

"You're shameless," I say as I grab the milk from the fridge.

"Shouldn't you be asleep?" Patrick asks, startling me. The jug of milk almost slips through my fingers.

"You need lessons on how to make a sound when you walk so you can stop sneaking up on me," I say as I crouch down and pour the milk into the bowl.

"Where would be the fun in that?" Patrick asks, rolling his shoulders. His eyes are bright, his hair is mussed, and he's practically bouncing on his toes.

"How much did you eat?" I ask, raising a brow.

"So much," Patrick grins. "Reilly suggested I drink more than I usually would, just for the next couple of weeks."

I shake my head, though I can't help smiling. "You're going to be blood-drunk for a week? God help us all."

"Speaking of drunk, Emilio put tequila in the pantry for you."

"He did?" I ask, perking up and heading straight for the pantry, pulling the door open and scanning the shelves. "Where is it?"

Patrick reaches around me and snags it off the top shelf. "You're worse with alcohol than your cat is with her treats."

"I am not!" I object as I unscrew the bottle and take a swig. It burns, but Emilio got some top notch stuff, so it's also smooth as tequila can get.

A couple of neckers walk by the kitchen, whispering when they see us.

"Let's go sit outside," I say, already walking toward the back door. Patrick jogs after me.

We walk out into the back yard, past the weird little garden of night blooming plants, and into the maze of hedges. My breath puffs out in little clouds as we walk.

I take another swig, choosing random directions until I think I might actually be lost. The tequila already has my head feeling fuzzy.

"You sure you should be drinking that much before the funeral?"

I stop and throw a glare over my shoulder. "I think I can decide for myself, thanks."

Patrick raises his hands in front of his chest. "Just making sure."

"You normally encourage bad behavior and decisions. Who even are you?" I plop down on the ground, leaning back against the hedge. The leaves are prickly and cold. I shiver and take another drink to warm up.

"I don't even know anymore," Patrick says, sitting down beside me and resting his head on my shoulder. He looks at the bottle enviously. "I wish I could drink tequila still."

"Ugh, remind me to never become a vampire. If I couldn't have tequila, I'd rather be true dead than undead and immortal."

Patrick snorts.

We sit quietly for a few minutes. I stare up at the sky, spinning the bottle listlessly between my fingers.

"Did I ever tell you why I chose to take the bite?" Patrick asks, picking at the seam of his jeans.

"No." I set the bottle down between my legs. "Why did you?"

"I was sick all the time. Not anything serious, just a cold that would always turn into bronchitis, and sometimes pneumonia. Or the flu. Or whatever might be going around." He shrugs and readjusts his head on my shoulder. "I was just sick and weak and useless."

"And you wanted to be a strong, immortal vampire instead?"

"I suppose," he says, spreading his hands. "I'm not sure exactly what I expected. I definitely thought it would be more glamorous. It might have been, I guess. If the vampire in the city I was living in had accepted my request, it could have been everything I imagined."

"They turned you down?" I take another sip.

"They laughed me out of the clanhouse. Said they didn't need a weak, pathetic human in their clan."

I snort. "Assholes."

"Yeah, we're something," he sighs, slipping his arm through mine. His skin doesn't put off the same heat a human's would. He's useless for staying warm out here.

"How'd you meet Javier, then?"

"I got desperate and started contacting every clan within three hundred miles. Javier invited me here for an interview." Patrick laughs. "It was so strange, but he was dead serious. He made me meet everyone, asked all sorts of intrusive questions, then offered me the bite on the spot. Said it was now or never, and I didn't even hesitate."

"Do you regret it?" I ask, something uncomfortable twisting in my chest as I remember his face twisted in hunger and spit dripping from his chin as he latched onto my arm in that basement. And the night before last, when his hunger almost overtook him again.

He twists so his forehead is resting on my shoulder and wraps his hand around my arm. "This week I have. I never thought it would turn me into a murderer."

"You're not a murderer," I say, almost harshly. "You're not."

He shakes his head, his breath hitching. "You don't know what it's like to kill someone. You can't understand."

I laugh, a humorless sound, and my eyes sting. I squeeze them shut and take another drink.

"Yes, I do."

He lifts his head. "What are you talking about?"

"The first person I killed was a vampire," I whisper as I grab the neck of my shirt and pull it to the side to show him the faint scars I could never get to disappear entirely. "Got obsessed and tried to kill me."

Patrick traces the scar with a cold fingertip and looks at me with tired eyes. "I'm surprised you don't hate us."

"I almost did," I say with a smile. "I was terrified when I started here. Only took the job because I was desperate as hell."

"You said the first person you killed?" he asks quietly. "Have there been more?"

I pull my arm away and stand; I've already said too much. Damn tequila.

"What happened to your neck?" I ask, pointing to the bruise on the side closest to me. His hand goes to it, and he shrugs, looking almost embarrassed.

"I left the clan; coming back wasn't as simple as just walking back in the house."

"Javier didn't hurt you, did he?" I demand, tugging at his hand to get a better look.

"No," he says, taking my wrists in his hands to keep me from pawing at his neck. "It wasn't like that."

"What was it like, then?" I ask, sitting back and taking another drink.

"When a vampire joins a clan, there's a sharing of blood," he says, a blush creeping up his neck. I didn't even know vampires could blush. "Javier and I had to do that again, in the presence of the clan."

I stare at him, brows raised. "You people have the weirdest fucking rules."

"Tell me about it," he says with a harsh laugh.

We go quiet, and the silence makes my skin itch. Sitting and thinking is the last thing I need.

"Let's walk more."

He opens his mouth to argue, then snaps it shut and shakes his head.

"I'll race you to the center."

I grin, wide and manic, then take off at an unsteady sprint.

The room is still spinning from the tequila, and I'm starting to feel like I might barf. Fucking tequila. I stumble towards the dresser, fumbling through the vials Emilio lined up on top of it.

"Where are you?" I ask in a singsong voice. Don't need the blood replenishing potion, don't need the iron supplement potion, don't need the sweet dreams potion.

"There it is!" I exclaim as I find the little purple vial that contains the sobering potion I keep for emergencies. I flick the cork out and down it before I can hesitate.

I gag immediately and have to pinch my nose to swallow it back down. Disgusting doesn't cover it. It's bitter and salty and sour all at the same time. The potion rushes through me, chasing the alcohol out of my bloodstream and back into my stomach, which twists and cramps.

I run for the bathroom and fling the toilet lid open, vomiting three times before I can catch a breath. I'm pretty sure some came out of my nose.

"So gross," I groan. My stomach cramps again, and I vomit up the remaining tequila. With the haze of the alcohol gone, I just feel tired, and stupid.

I get a hand on the sink and pull myself up on shaky legs. Panting, and still nauseous, I brace myself and wait to see if I'm going to vomit again. My stomach cramps once more, but I don't vomit. I turn the water on and rinse my mouth out before grabbing my toothbrush.

It takes a couple of minutes of scrubbing to get the taste out of my mouth. I spit in the sink and make the mistake of looking in the mirror. I'm going to need a shit ton of makeup to make myself look presentable. First, though, I have to take a shower.

The hot water soothes my now sore muscles and eases the last of the cramping in my stomach. I want to linger, but it's already six-thirty, and the funeral is at eight am. I really can't be late, plus I don't think Lydia would wait for me, and I don't have a car anymore.

I sigh and lean my head against the shower wall. Tequila had helped me forget that little piece of information, and I could have done without remembering it. I slap the water off and grab the towel I put on the counter.

Fifteen minutes later, I have my one nice dress laid out. It's a navy blue, a-line dress that belonged to my mom. I smooth out a wrinkle and stare at it. I haven't ever worn it, but I couldn't ever bear to get rid of it. I don't have many of her things left, just an old cauldron I can't even use anymore, and this. I shake off the memories and pull the dress on. It fits like a glove.

I blow dry my hair and twist it up into a bun. Then I slather on the concealer and foundation followed by a little blush to put some color on my cheeks so I don't look like a vampire. Finally, I put on mascara to make myself look awake. It's the closest I can get to reputable looking.

Standing there, looking in the mirror, all I can see is my mother. She looked almost exactly like this every time she went to deal with coven business. The welts striping my arms ruin the image though. The salves haven't been helping at all. I touch one; it's still tender, and I can feel the tingle of magic still running through it. I shove down the worry over what exactly I've done to myself and pull on a long sleeve cardigan to hide them.

My phone buzzes. Lydia is asking if I'm ready, or if she's going to have to come drag me out of bed. I text back that I'm headed down, then grab my purse, stuffed full of potions because you can never be too careful, and a light jacket.

Lydia, who is waiting at the bottom of the stairs, looks perfect, of course. She's wearing a tailored black dress with a string of pearls, her hair in a perfect chignon. The dress softens her broad shoulders, and her makeup makes her look both younger, and more somber than usual.

"I'm glad you had something decent to wear. I almost had Emilio get you something, just in case."

"Oh, ye of little faith," I say, adjusting my skirt as I come to a stop in front of her. I feel awkward in a dress.

Lydia crosses her arms like she's preparing for a

fight. "All right, just so you know, the coven is going to be there, and they aren't happy you're attending. Novak's girlfriend, however, is human and insisted that you be permitted to attend. She's been insisting on meeting the witch her boyfriend died to protect."

"Great," I say, going to rub a hand across my face, then thinking better of it. I drop my hand to my side. "I'm not great with comforting people."

"Just tell her he was your hero, and don't crack any jokes. You'll be fine."

"Sure," I say.

Lydia looks unconvinced but heads to the garage regardless. She's driving one of Javier's sleek black cars today. The leather squeaks as I try to find a comfortable position.

We're almost to the cemetery when Lydia interrupts the silence.

"I got an email from Agent Hawking this morning."

"They found something?" I demand, sitting up straighter.

"Perhaps," Lydia shrugs. "It's a very tentative lead, but they think they have Martinez on a security camera at a gas station about fifty miles from here."

I clench my fingers around the strap of my purse. I want to find him so bad, I can taste it. Suddenly, Reilly extorting me into helping doesn't seem so bad.

"That's something."

Lydia nods. "It certainly is."

She turns down the narrow lane that leads through the cemetery. The parking lot is already full of cars with a stream of people walking toward the canopy tent set up over the gravesite.

Lydia parks at the back of the parking lot. I get out and smooth my dress down. I'm not sure how my mother ever sat in it without wrinkling it.

I see a few familiar faces as I walk up. Some I've simply seen around town, others are in pressed blue uniforms. A narrow black strip with the words *nemo me impune lacessit* stretches across their badges. They did the same at Brunson's funeral, from what I saw in the pictures.

"It means 'No one harms me with impunity',' Lydia says, seeing my stare.

"That's a good motto," I say as we near the canopy. There aren't many seats left open. Novak's family has filled the front row, the police the second and third, and the coven most of the rest. However, there is one face missing I expected to see.

"Wasn't Maybelle supposed to be here?" I whisper as we take a seat in the back corner. The chairs are rickety plastic here in the back, and it squeaks as I sit down.

Lydia glances around discretely, brows pinching together. "She was."

A hush settles over the gathering. The minister steps up to a podium behind the casket and clears his throat.

"We are here today to honor a fallen hero, a dear friend, and a distinguished member of the Ignatius Coven and Pecan Grove Police Department, Alexander Novak. He was not only a police officer, nor was he only a witch, nor was he only a son. Alexander was a part of this community, and a good man who stood ready to defend this town against the greatest threat of our time."

I stare at my hands, clenched tightly together. Novak threatened me. He tampered with evidence at the request of the coven leader. But in the end, he came down into a basement to try and stop his partner, and he died trying to do the right thing.

"We are here today to lay this man to rest surrounded by the community he cared so much for," the minister continues. "Surrounded by the family that loved him, and his fiancée, whose future with him has been cut short. We are all here seeking comfort, which we will find in each other. Each of us mourns the loss of Alexander, and we will continue to mourn. I encourage you to lean on one other."

His fiancée is sobbing audibly now. His mother and father are staring straight ahead, eyes locked on the casket. I shouldn't be allowed here. I shouldn't be sitting at the funeral of a man I killed watching the people who cared about him grieve. It wasn't my fault, really, that he died, but I still sucked him dry and felt his soul slip from his body.

I dig my nails into my palm just to keep myself in my seat. The minister drones on. Lydia nudges me, and I realize I've been tapping my foot. I still and take a deep breath.

Three officers line up to the left, shotguns held at their sides. A fourth officer stands apart from them. He clicks his heels together, standing at attention.

"Firing squad. Attention!" His voice echoes across the space.

The other officers snap to attention as well.

"Ready. Aim. Fire."

The three shots crack through the air simultaneously. I flinch, digging my nails into my palm even deeper.

"Ready. Aim. Fire."

The shots crack again. I force myself to look up.

"Ready. Aim. Fire."

The final shot sounds, the report of gunfire echoing into the distance.

"Present arms."

The officer lifts a trumpet and begins playing taps. As the somber tune carries over the gathering,

Novak's mother finally breaks down, tears streaming down her face.

The minister says a few more words, but I don't hear them. Lydia's hand on my arm startles me, and I realize they are finally lowering the casket. She presses the keys to the car into my hand and leans in to whisper in my ear.

"I'll get a ride back to the clanhouse from someone else."

I grip the keys tightly and nod. I'm the first person out of my seat, and it's all I can do to keep from sprinting to the car. I don't see Brunson and Hawking until I'm rushing past them. Zachary's eyes follow me, that same tired look on his face from the last time we spoke. This must be even harder for him than it is for me, yet I'm still the one running away.

13

I drive exactly the speed limit on the way into town, even though I want to rush. I'm almost desperate to see Maybelle at this point. There are too many unanswered questions, and if I can't do something productive, I think I might go crazy. I could also use some good news about rebuilding the apothecary.

The cafe is almost empty. It's unheard of, and it makes my heart twist in my chest. Even the lights seem dimmer today.

I adjust my dress and wish I had thought to bring a change of clothes. I hadn't really planned for after the funeral though.

"Olivia," a familiar voice says from behind me.

I turn around and click my jaw shut after a moment. I've never seen Gerard out of the warehouse before. He looks even paler in the light, and he doesn't seem to like it based on the angry squint twisting his features.

"Gerard?" I ask dumbly.

He rolls his eyes and huffs. "You aren't normally this stupid. But yes."

I glare at him. "I've never seen you outside the warehouse. It's weird. What do you want?"

"Maybelle has been taken," he says, baring his teeth. "Find her."

I swallow. My mind is running in a million directions. Does he know? Who has taken Maybelle? I curl my hands into fists. I don't know if I could stand it if someone else died.

"Who took her?"

"It doesn't matter," he says, shaking his head. "You find her, and you get her back."

I pull my phone out of my purse. "Is this related to the bombing? Do you know who did it?"

He closes the distance between us in four quick steps, snatching my phone from my hand. I didn't realize he was capable of moving that fast.

"You call no one, and tell no one," he bites out. "If she's still alive, she'll not thank you for ruining her life by involving JHAPI."

"How do you know any of this? And why do you care?" I ask, taken aback by his vehemence.

"Because," he hisses, "she's my sister."

"Your *sister*?" I demand, leaning toward and speaking in a low voice. "Is this some kind of joke?"

"We are private people," Gerard says, crossing his arms. "You can demand all the answers you want after you find her."

"Why do you think she has been taken?" I ask, narrowing my eyes at him.

He thrusts a crumpled note in my face. I snatch it and smooth it out to read it.

What was stolen must be returned. Your sister for the book. You have forty-eight hours.

. . .

I look back up at Gerard, my brow furrowed. "What was stolen? A book?"

"It doesn't matter," he says, thrusting a finger at me. "We sold it years ago, and we can't get it back. They will kill her if we don't find her first."

"This is insane," I snap. Of course I'm going to try to Find her, but none of this makes sense. "When did you get this note?"

"Midnight the day of the explosion."

"Shit, so we're already down, what, twenty-four hours?"

He nods.

"You should have asked for help sooner," I say in a barely controlled tone of voice.

"I couldn't get to you without giving everything away. You have been surrounded by the vampires almost constantly since the bombing," he hisses at me. "It would have done neither of us any good."

I brush a stray piece of hair out of my face roughly. "This is insanity."

"It's only a matter of time before they come for you as well. I'm surprised they haven't made the connection already," he says, shaking his head.

"What connection? I apparently don't know anything about Maybelle," I say, waving the note at him.

"That's for her to tell you," he says. He's already backing away.

"Why are you always so damn vague?" I snap. "Just give me a straight answer."

"I know what you are, and what you can do. Find Maybelle, or I tell the vampire," Gerard says evenly. His shoulders are hunched up by his ears, and his hands are curled into fists like he's ready for a fight.

I glare at him, my heart in my throat and the note crumpling in my clenched hand. I clench my teeth to keep from yelling at him or threatening him. I want to find Maybelle even if I do hate him right now.

"Do you have a map?" I grit out.

"At the warehouse," he says, turning and walking away. I lock the car and follow.

Gerard's office is in even more disarray than usual. The chair is knocked over, and one of the computer screens is dangling from the wall, held up only by the cord. I stand in the doorway while he digs through a drawer and pulls out several maps.

"I don't think they've taken her far," he explains as he pulls a map partially open, then tosses it to the side and keeps digging.

"Why do you think that?" I ask, my thumb brushing over the worst of the welts on my hand. I want to itch it, but I know I would regret it.

"They think she still has it. That she has just hidden it somewhere," he says. He opens another map, nods, and brings it to me.

"But she doesn't?" I ask, taking the map with both hands.

"No." Gerard shakes his head wearily. "It would be easier if we did though. These people can't be reasoned with."

"Is it the NWR?"

He laughs, though there is no humor to the sound. "I wish."

"You or Maybelle are going to tell me everything after I find her," I say before I begin. "Especially why you think I might be next."

"If you really want to know," Gerard agrees begrudgingly.

"I do."

I brush past him, dump my purse on the ground, and spread the map out on his desk. It's a map of the county. Just large enough to ensure that I'll find her if she's here, but small enough that there's less chance I'll overexert myself.

The welts on my hand are starting to show through the concealer I put on them, probably because I've rubbed my hands too much today. I curl my fingers under and focus on the map.

The paper is dusty as I smooth my hands over it. I shut my eyes and nudge the Finding magic. It responds almost eagerly. I breathe a sigh of relief and push harder, picturing Maybelle's face in my mind as I search. Red lines wind down from my hands, scattering across the map like a spider web. She's close. Still in the town, but I can't see where yet, I can't—

A wave of pain hits me in the gut, and it feels like the welts are being burned into my skin all over again. My hands twitch on the map as I try to pull the magic back. It won't stop.

Olivia.

I gasp and try to open my eyes, but I can't seem to move. It feels like I'm falling.

Olivia.

I can hear her voice like she's right behind me. The burning pain in my arms doubles, and I think I might be screaming, but I can't hear anything but my own labored breathing and the frantic beating of my heart.

My head and back hit something hard. The air rushes from my lungs. My body shakes as my muscles contract violently.

I can see my mother standing over me, but I can't reach her.

14

My hand twitches spastically. I can see it from the corner of my eye, but I can't make it stop. I can't seem to move at all.

The cardigan I'm wearing is scorched and falling to pieces on my arm. The welts, now an even darker red and inflamed, show through the gaps.

Another spasm wracks my body, and I grunt in pain, but I'm able to move my fingers. I focus on that, forcing my first finger, and then my second to curl in toward my palm. One by one, I coerce each muscle to move and roll onto my side.

I can't hear anyone in the room. Gerard must have abandoned me like this. I lift my head, the room spins for a moment, then comes back into focus. He's gone, the asshole. I guess he decided since I failed at Finding Maybelle, I wasn't worth fooling with anymore.

I groan and push myself upright and lean back against the wall. It takes a second to catch my breath. I rip the cardigan off and touch the shoulder of the dress tentatively. It's ruined. The welts are much worse as well. And not just that, they've spread.

I brush my hand from my shoulder up my neck

and feel the welts stop just above my collarbone. Based on the ache in my chest and side, I think they may have extended there as well.

My phone rings. I stare at my purse and consider just letting it go to voicemail, but as it rings again, I sigh and push myself onto my knees and crawl to my purse.

The caller ID says it's Lydia. I answer and put the phone to my ear.

"Hey, Lydia," I say hoarsely. It hurts to speak.

"Olivia, you need to come to your house," Lydia says, her voice tight.

"Why?" I ask, trying to keep my voice steady despite the pain shooting through my side and the growing headache pounding in the back of my head.

"Your house was broken into," Lydia hesitates before continuing. "Nothing was taken that we can tell, but there has been some damage."

I want to sink into the floor and never get up. My heart twists when I think about what could have happened to Mr. Muffins if I hadn't decided to stay with the vampires.

"How much damage?" I ask finally.

"Slurs on the door and some of the walls. Some things have been broken. Your workroom is the worst. I think the ingredients will be unusable."

"And this was done by…" I trail off. I don't want to say their name. *His* name.

"It does look like something the NWR would do, though there is no evidence Martinez is back."

I look down at my still trembling hands, the red welts darker and inflamed. I have no choice. I can't do this on my own.

"Maybelle has gone missing. She left a note you may want to read before we talk to the police."

"Where are you?" Lydia demands. I can hear her heels snapping against a wood floor.

"The warehouse. Gerard's."

"What—" She cuts herself off. "Stay there, I'm sending someone to get you."

"You can't," I object. "Only you. No one else, not until we talk."

"Olivia, it's been almost five hours since you ran away from the funeral. Special Agent Hawking was already starting to get concerned something had happened to you. There will be questions."

"I'm sure you can help me think up a good excuse." I let my head thunk back against the wall. "I also need a change of clothes."

One of the computer screens flares to life, almost blinding me. I squint into the sudden light and realize it's showing Lydia opening the door.

"Olivia?" Lydia shouts from the front of the warehouse.

"In the back!" I shout back, which sends me into a coughing fit. It's dusty in here, and I desperately need some water.

She shuts the door, and the computer screen goes dark once again. That explains why Gerard was never surprised to see me at least.

Lydia's heels echo loudly as she walks to the back room. I don't bother trying to stand. The door to Gerard's office swings open. Lydia is wearing a low cut red dress with a ruffled skirt and glittery black heels. Her gray hair swings around her face in soft curls.

"What—were you on a date?" I ask, mouth hanging open.

"I'm old, not dead, Olivia," she says, chunking a bag of clothes at my head. I only manage to half-block it and barely keep it from dropping onto the dirty floor.

"Thanks." I dig through the bag, relieved to see a long sleeved shirt. I'd forgotten to specify.

"What the hell happened to you? Are those burns?" Lydia says, concern tinging her voice as she comes closer, crouching down next to me.

"I think they are," I say with a shrug. "Help me up?"

She grasps my hand and pulls me up quickly. My legs tremble, but I don't collapse.

"Olivia," she says, hands on hips. "What is going on?"

I turn away from her and strip my dress off. She gasps as it falls away. My back must look even worse than it feels.

"Magic is temperamental sometimes. I made a mistake the other day that I'm still paying for," I explain as I dig the jeans out of the bag.

"What did you do?" she asks firmly.

I pull the shirt on and tug the sleeves as far down over my hands as I can. If I'm lucky, and if no one looks too carefully, I might be able to get away with it.

"Olivia, don't ignore me," she snaps.

I turn around, suddenly angry. Angry I have to ask for help. Angry Gerard put me in the position. Angry I've made so many stupid decisions in a row.

"They'll kill me, Lydia, or find a way to use me," I snap back. "I don't know which is worse, but I don't want to find out."

"You can trust me—"

"No, I can't," I say, curling my arms around myself. "If I told you, you would have to tell Javier. I know you can't lie to him, and he's your employer anyhow. The only reason you're helping me at all is because he told you to."

Lydia takes a deep breath and looks at me steadily. "That is true, but you are useful to Javier. He would want to protect you."

Her honesty hurts more than it should. *Useful.* That's what I've been reduced to. All of my struggling and pain and all the risks I have taken for Javier can be summed up in one word. I knew all of this, but I guess some childish, fanciful part of me still cared. I should know better by now than to get attached.

"If you want me to keep being useful to Javier, then forget what you saw and don't ask me about it again."

Lydia pinches the bridge of her nose, considering. "Javier may not take no for an answer. What you do after that will be up to you."

I groan aloud and run my fingers through my hair. "Did you know Gerard was Maybelle's brother?"

"What?" Lydia asks, thrown off by the abrupt subject change.

I thrust the note toward her.

"Gerard brought me this and asked for my help Finding her. He didn't want the police involved."

Lydia takes the note, reading it silently. She looks up finally and hands the note back to me. I can see the wheels turning in her head; she knows I shouldn't be able to use that kind of magic. She knows I found Patrick. She probably knows about Aaron Hall lying in this very warehouse last week. I had asked Javier to clean up that mess for me after all. That was sloppy.

"As your lawyer, I have to advise you to take this to the police," she says. "Did you Find her?"

"No, I passed out. Gerard left while I was unconscious."

She turns and paces the small, cleared area in the middle of Gerard's office. "The note said forty-eight hours?"

I nod and tug on the ends of my sleeves again. The material of the shirt feels like sandpaper on the welts, even though it's fairly soft.

"Then you have to tell them," Lydia says, coming to a stop. "We can't risk waiting and trying to find her ourselves."

"She didn't want the police involved."

"Did she tell you that, or did Gerard?" Lydia asks.

I gnaw on the inside of my cheek. "Gerard."

"Can he be trusted? Is he even actually her brother?"

I put my head back in my hands. "I don't know."

I feel utterly lost. I cared about Maybelle, someone else who apparently has secrets. Gerard could be playing me somehow. I have no idea if he's out to get Maybelle or help her. He seemed sincere and desperate when he came to get my help. Well, to force me to help him.

"Come see your house, perhaps that will help you decide," Lydia says, hands on hips.

"Is it that bad?"

"Whatever you think, it's probably worse."

15

As we approach the house the first thing I can see is the fluorescent red scrawl of *BLOODBAG* and *WHORE* across the front of the house.

"I can see they wanted to keep it subtle," I mutter. Lydia snorts and parks the car behind the police car and the unmarked black car I recognize as Brunson's.

"Just wait 'til you see the inside," she says with a shake of her head.

We climb out of the car, and I take a deep breath to steady the sudden churning in my stomach. I have felt unsettled since we left the warehouse, and the feeling has only gotten worse on the way here.

Brunson meets us on the front porch.

"What happened to you?" he asks, looking me up and down, brows furrowed.

"Nothing, I just changed clothes," I say with a tight-lipped smile.

"There's dirt on your face," he says, pointing at my cheek. I rub at the spot he pointed at with my sleeve.

"Just let me inside. I need to see how bad the workroom is."

He turns and pushes the door open for me. It swings unsteadily on the hinges. The doorknob is more or less dangling from the door, and the latch is completely busted off.

Inside is chaos. Every cabinet has been flung open, the contents strewn across the floor. A jar of cherries is broken in the middle of the kitchen. Sticky red syrup is splashed all over the cabinets like a murder scene. A carton of eggs is upside down in front of the refrigerator. My last bottle of whiskey is broken too. Assholes.

The table is flipped over, one chair is broken, and the other is lying on its side. The couch is ripped open, and the stuffing has been shredded and scattered around the room like snow. I feel numb. It doesn't even look like my house anymore.

I step over a dented can of green beans and walk through the kitchen and living room, absently noting they broke the television as well. The window unit is lying face down on the floor surrounded by glass. There are random holes in the walls. The edges of the carpet have been pulled up in various places.

The workroom door is shut, and I hesitate before I push it open. I should have left it closed. The chest of herbs is upended. Perfectly good ingredients are ground into the floor, wilted and smashed. Two of the cauldrons are fine, but the copper one is dented beyond repair. These were things that touched something inside of me no person ever has. It feels like my heart is lying trampled on the floor.

Every drawer has been pulled open, but one, in particular, catches my eye. It's empty. The crystals are gone.

I hear someone come to a stop in the hall behind me and glance back. It's Hawking; I hadn't even realized she was here.

"They took my crystals," I comment.

"Crystals?"

"Yeah, stuff like azurite or citrine. Everything in that drawer," I say, pointing it out. "Just odd since they didn't take anything else. At least nothing I've noticed so far."

"Any idea what they were looking for so intently?" Hawking asks, crossing her arms and leaning against the door jamb.

"I really don't." I shake my head. "I don't have anything worth all this. The only things of value were in here, and they didn't even take the most expensive things."

"What are the most expensive things?"

"Just the cauldrons, they're solid metal," I say, waving a hand at them. "They're not rare though. Some of the crystals were, I guess, or at least hard to get."

"And who got them for you?"

"Gerard."

Hawking scratches a few notes down. "Got a last name?"

"Not that I know of." I shrug. "He's a little odd. Doesn't like to give out personal information."

"All right, let me know if you see anything else missing," Hawking says before walking back toward the living room.

I nudge a fallen vial with my foot. It's cracked but not completely shattered, which is good considering it's deoxygenation potion. I press the palms of my hands against my eyes as I try to process all the things I'm going to have to replace.

"You smell like fire, and old Chinese food," Reilly says.

I jump and turn around, almost stepping on the vial when I see he is standing right behind me now. He grabs my shoulders and steadies me. I bite down on a wince. I need to get back to the clanhouse soon.

The salves I have may not be able to heal these marks, but it does keep them from hurting so much.

"You have got to stop doing that," I say, shrugging his hands away.

"Perhaps when it stop amusing me," he smirks. My eyes stray to his dimples and the curl of hair sticking out from behind his ear.

"Where have you been?" he asks.

I jerk my eyes away from him and look around the room instead.

"At a funeral," I step around him.

"Whoever did this were witches," he says, looking around the room with his hands in his pockets, jacket pushed back. He's wearing his usual suit, but he didn't put on a tie today. The first couple of buttons of his shirt are undone; he looks like he dressed in a rush. "I can smell the magic."

"Of course it smells like magic in here," I say slowly, raising a brow. "I brew here."

"I know what your magic smells like," he says, stalking toward me. "It smells like copper and fire and herbs and blood."

I take a step back, but he's faster. He crowds me against the wall by the door, one hand on either side of my head. His eyes are so blue, they almost glow up this close. My heartbeat is picking up, but I can't claim it's all from fear.

"These people smell strange, like dust and mildew. Their magic is colder as well."

"Are you seriously trying to pin this on the coven?" I ask with a huff. "I know McGuinness hates me, but I don't think he'd go to this much trouble to ruin my day."

Reilly shakes his head. "No, it wasn't the local coven, but it was a coven."

"So, a coven trashed my house, and the NWR

blew up the apothecary?" I ask, crossing my arms over my chest to keep the space between us.

"Oh no," he says, taking a step back finally. "The people who trashed your house are the same ones who planted the bomb."

I bite the inside of my cheek. The note left after Maybelle's disappearance definitely didn't seem the like NWR. I'm not sure if that should reassure me or not.

"That would explain Maybelle's disappearance and the note that was left, I guess," I say flatly.

"What note?" Brunson asks, appearing in the doorway.

I pull it out of my back pocket and hand it to him. "Where's Agent Hawking? I only want to have to explain this once."

I slip past Brunson and walk to the living room, where I can hear Hawking and Lydia talking. He and Reilly follow close behind. I grab one of the overturned chairs and right it, then sit down heavily, my legs stretched out in front of me.

"Where did you get this?"

"Gerard gave it to me and demanded I help him find Maybelle," I say, crossing my arms. "He didn't want to get the police involved, but I can't find her on my own."

"What else did he tell you?" Brunson demands.

"He said she was his sister." I look down to avoid the glare Brunson has focused on me.

"Interesting," Reilly says. "Maybelle seems not to have been very forthcoming at all."

"Has Maybelle ever hinted that Gerard was family?" Hawking asks.

"No, not in the slightest. She wasn't even the one to recommend Gerard to me as a supplier for my potion ingredients."

"Who was?" Brunson asks.

"Javier," I say with a shrug. "He said Gerard had gotten him something in the past."

"Any idea what?" Brunson asks, looking between me and Lydia.

"Blood replenishing potions for the people the clan feeds on," Lydia says. "Now Olivia supplies them for us."

"Is it possible they were searching your house for this book as well?"

"I guess, but I have no idea why they would." I shrug. "I'm connected to Maybelle and Gerard, but I've known them both for less than a year."

"So this note was left for Gerard?" Hawking asks, reaching for it. Brunson hands it to her, and she reads it carefully, flipping it over and examining the edges. She sniffs it carefully and grimaces.

"That's what he said." I shrug. It hadn't occurred to me before, but every partnership in JHAPI consists of a human and a paranormal. Hawking must be a werewolf.

"Can you get anything off this other than Olivia and dust?" Hawking asks, handing the note to Reilly.

He takes it and sniffs it carefully, turning the slip of paper over and sniffing that side as well. I press my lips together to keep the sudden urge to laugh under control. It just makes for such a ridiculous image.

"There's some scent I have smelled before but can't place," Reilly says, frowning. "There is a hint of whoever came here as well."

"We should go to Maybelle's house, see if we can find any trace the people who came here," Hawking says to Brunson. "If they're connected, that makes it even less likely the NWR is behind any of this."

"I'll give Olivia a ride and meet you there," Reilly says, striding toward me.

Hawking nods and pulls keys out of her pocket.

"I need to go update Javier," Lydia says. "I'll see you back at the clanhouse, Olivia."

I nod and follow Reilly outside. He is parked behind Lydia, apparently having borrowed one of Javier's sporty red convertibles.

I slide into the passenger seat, the leather squeaking as I try to get comfortable. It still has that new car smell, even though I know Javier bought this right around the time I started working for him. What a waste.

Reilly folds himself into the driver seat, which is pushed back as far as it will go. The car rumbles to life, and Reilly puts it in reverse and whips around. I grab the door handle and glare at him.

"It's not a race," I snap.

"No point in wasting time though." He grins. "It would be convenient to get there before the agents as well."

He doesn't slow down for any of the sharp turns. The car hugs the road, but I always feel uneasy when other people drive. It doesn't help knowing that Reilly could walk away from a wreck that would kill me.

"Why did Gerard think you could find his sister?" Reilly asks.

I grip the door handle tighter. "I found Patrick. I suppose he thought I could do it again."

"But you couldn't?" Reilly asks, turning his head to look at me.

"Watch the road." I reach out and push his chin back forward. His skin is warmer than I expected, much like his mouth was. I swallow and abruptly cut off that line of thinking. "And no, I couldn't."

Not a lie, but I'm sure my heartbeat is giving me away. Maybe he'll just attribute it to some kind of twisted attraction to him.

"You really do smell odd," he says, leaning over to sniff me again.

"Don't do that." I reach out to shove him away, but he takes a sharp turn and I am thrown into his side instead. I might smell odd, but he smells amazing. His cologne is warm and masculine, and I have a sudden urge to bury my face in the curve of his shoulder. I sit up and settle back in my seat instead. Anyone over the age of thirteen shouldn't blush, but I can still feel my cheeks heating up. I hate him so much.

"You're a terrible driver," I complain. "Can you try being a decent driver for a little while?"

"And stop giving you excuses to cuddle with me?" he says with a grin. His stupid dimples make him look innocent, but I know it's all a facade. "You do jump into my arms every chance you get."

"Walking into you because you don't understand personal space is *not* the same thing, asshole," I say, crossing my arms. I flinch when I hit a welt on the side of my arm more forcefully than I intended. My shirt dampens over the spot, and I'm not sure if it a blister popped, or if I'm bleeding. I glance at Reilly from the corner of my eye.

"The answer is yes," he says without looking at me.

"What?"

"I can smell that you are hurt." He downshifts, revving the engine as we take another turn far too fast. "And you will tell me why, eventually."

I huff and turn toward the window. The trees thin out, and we reach the edges of town. My stomach aches less than it did, but the discomfort has been replaced with irritation and worry.

He turns into a subdivision I've never driven through before. It's a little out of the way, but still close to town. Halfway into the subdivision, Reilly pulls into the driveway of a particularly nice house. It's slightly larger than the others and perfectly maintained.

Maybelle's house looks untouched. The door is shut, the blinds drawn, the freshly mowed lawn undisturbed. There are no slurs painted across her perfect, white shutters. It looks like everyone's favorite grandmother's house, just as I expected.

Reilly parks, and we climb out. I tug my sleeves down again, but the ache in my arms is getting worse. I wish I could have put salve on the burns before coming here.

Reilly inhales deeply then in the time it takes me to blink is halfway across the front lawn. I frown and hurry after him.

"Do you smell anything?" I ask.

He ignores me and opens the front door. I follow him inside and see that Maybelle's house is trashed even worse than mine was. Everything that could be ripped apart is.

Reilly turns around slowly, inhaling deeply, his mouth pulled into a frown.

"I should have recognized it on the note," he says, tone irritated.

"Recognized what?"

"The same witches that trashed your house were here," he says, turning to look at me. "But there have also been goblins here."

"Goblins?" I say, confused. "They never leave their cities."

"Apparently, they do."

The door opens behind us.

"Apparently, they do what?" Hawking asks, eager blue eyes darting between us. She stops, her mouth opening slightly as she inhales. "What is that smell? It's almost reptilian."

"It's proof Maybelle is a liar," Reilly says, his eyes never leaving mine. He smiles, cheeks dimpling.

I turn away, frustration and irritation coursing through me.

16

He parks right in front of the house, and I shove the car door open, practically jumping out. I'm tired of being trapped in that car with him.

"The smell isn't superficial either. It's part of the house. However long Maybelle has been there, the goblin has been as well," Reilly says as we walk up the steps to the clanhouse. "Hawking agreed."

"There has to be something we're missing. She can't be a goblin," I say, aghast.

"Do you have any other explanations?" he asks, stepping toward me. There isn't even a hint of a smile on his face; he seems almost angry.

"A goblin could have visited her, even lived with her," I say, taking a step back from Reilly.

"Use your head," he says, poking my forehead, "and not your heart."

He presses his finger over my heart a little more gently.

I slap his hand away.

"I am," I snap. "You're just jumping to conclusions. If Maybelle is a goblin, why does she look human?"

"There are Enchanters that have successfully made objects that are capable of disguising someone."

I scoff. "For it to disguise her appearance all day, every day would be an insane amount of magic."

"I have seen more powerful magic used," he says, crossing his arms. "It's not impossible, and it's the simplest explanation."

"And Gerard? He says he's her brother."

Reilly's head tilts to the side. "I need to smell you again."

"I'm sorry, what?"

He doesn't respond, just walks toward me. I shuffle backward and bump into the railing. I reach back to steady myself on instinct, and Reilly presses his hands over mine on the railing. His thighs brush mine as he leans in. He lowers his head, his cheek right next to mine, and breathes deeply.

I'm frozen, my heart beating wildly and crawling up my cheeks. I hate that he's my type and that I can even be considering something like this when Maybelle is missing. My body doesn't care though; it just wants him to lean in closer. It's been way too long since I've gotten laid or had any *alone time*.

"You smell like goblin here, and here," he says, lifting his hand from mine and brushing a finger across my shoulder, and my arm. "Did Gerard touch you?"

"Yes," I mutter. "Fuck."

It's impossible to deny at this point. The only question now is just, why? Why is she hiding here? She's been lying about who and what she is for years, and apparently hiding from some very powerful witches. That isn't something you do on a whim.

"If you want," Reilly says, pulling back just enough to look down at me. His lips are inches away.

It would be so easy to just forget all of this for an hour. Sex is almost better than tequila for dealing with a bad day.

"You all right, Olivia?" Patrick asks from the doorway.

I jump and tug my hand out from under Reilly's. He steps back, and I hurry toward Patrick.

"I'm great, just fine," I say as I walk quickly inside. Reilly chuckles behind me. He's going to be unforgivably smug about that.

Patrick looks between us, shakes his head, and follows me inside. Reilly's phone rings, and he pauses just inside the doorway and answers it.

I get halfway to the kitchen when Patrick's hand closes around my elbow. He drags me to the back door, then pushes me outside.

"What are you doing?" he asks, voice tight with anger.

"Looking for Maybelle," I say, jerking my elbow out of his grip. "What the fuck is your problem?"

"You know you can't trust him," Patrick hisses. "But you were about to stick your tongue down his throat like some kind of horny teenager."

"I was not!" I whisper back heatedly.

"I've been out with you enough to know that look," Patrick sneers. "You can lie to yourself, but don't lie to me."

"You know what? It's none of your business," I say, pushing past him and grabbing the door handle.

"I'm trying to help you," Patrick says, throwing his hands in the air in exasperation.

"Nah, you just think I'm a slut."

I yank the door open and walk back inside, slamming it behind me. I head straight for the kitchen. I need something, anything, to drink. Javier and Lydia walk out of the dining room behind me.

"Olivia, did you find any information on who might have taken Maybelle?" Javier asks.

I stop and turn to face them, tucking my thumbs in my pockets to keep my hands from shaking.

"All we've found are more questions."

"What do you know about goblins?" Reilly asks, walking up behind me. He comes to a stop at my elbow.

"Goblins?" Javier asks, brows furrowed.

"It seems both Maybelle and Gerard are not who they have said they are," Reilly says, slipping his phone back into his pocket.

"Lydia explained that Gerard is claiming to be her brother," Javier says with a nod.

"Both Special Agent Hawking and I smelled the distinct scent of goblins at Maybelle's house. As I was telling Olivia, it's obvious that the person living there is the goblin. There is almost no trace of visitors. It seems Maybelle did not invite people over often."

"Did you find any information on who has taken her?" Lydia asks. "Is it possible she has simply run away?"

"She did not run away," I say vehemently. "You read the note."

"The same witches who were at Olivia's house were at hers," Reilly says.

"And it's not the local coven?" Javier asks.

"No." Reilly shakes his head. "They smelled off. They've been somewhere very old recently."

"None of this makes sense," Lydia says. "I've known Maybelle for years, and while we weren't friends, she was never involved in anything less than reputable."

"It's insane," I say. "She has built so much here, she would never leave it all behind willingly."

"We have another complication as well," Reilly says, looking at me. "I just got off the phone with

Agent Brunson. The JHAPI agents have been re-
viewing security footage for everything within a
hundred square miles. Apparently, the day Martinez
fled, there was a break in at a veterinarian's office
about sixty miles from here. Martinez stole medical
supplies, then fled."

My heart constricts painfully. "Do they know
where he went from there?"

"Not yet, but it's a start. We know he fled alone
and didn't receive help from the NWR right away,"
Reilly says. "JHAPI is planning a raid on several
known NWR locations, they want the council's
support."

"Has the council agreed?" Javier asks, his shoulder's tense.

"Not yet, but they will," Reilly says. "Olivia and I
will be part of the support team."

"What?" I turn on Reilly, jaw clenched tight.

"I told you when I came here that you would be
helping the council apprehend Martinez. That hasn't
changed."

"Maybelle has been kidnapped!" I object, my voice
raising. "I can't just leave before she is found."

"Then you better hope she's found within the next
few days, because we are leaving regardless," Reilly
says coolly.

The realization that they aren't going to be able to
help her hits me like a punch in the gut. They care
about finding Martinez, but not her. I'm going to
have to do this myself. Somehow.

The Internet, unsurprisingly, does not have many details on the finer points of using Finding magic,

much less what to do when you fuck it up. I lock my phone and roll over and groan into my pillow.

I have about twelve hours left. The police have no leads, no idea who might have taken her, and the only thing we have learned is that we know nothing about Maybelle. That no one does.

I sit up and grab the salve off my nightstand. My arms are aching again. The blisters are all gone now, but sometimes it still feels like the welts are growing. Thankfully, the nausea I've been struggling since the warehouse has been slowly fading over the last hour.

The salve is cold, especially in contrast to the heat the welts are putting off right now. I lift the arm and check my side. One of the welts winds down from the top of my shoulder to my ribcage under my arm.

The only option I have left to find Maybelle is to attempt the Finding magic again. I poke at the welt and wonder how much it will grow if I try again. I'm not even sure where to start, or what went wrong last time.

My stomach jerks suddenly, and I'm on my feet, halfway to the bathroom, when something hits the bedroom window. The tug in my gut wants me to walk toward the window. I press my hand to my stomach and realize this is the magic.

I run to the window and fling the curtains to the side. I yank on the cord, and the blinds fly up. Standing just by a hedge at the edge of the maze, barely concealed, is Gerard. He tosses another rock at the window and waves me down, then ducks back behind the hedge.

I grab a handful of various potions, tuck the gun into my waistband, and run out of the room. It's just past dawn, and everyone else is asleep. Lydia left over an hour ago. I really hope this isn't a trap, but I know Maybelle is out there. I can feel it. The Finding magic had worked somehow, just not like it should have.

I shut the back door behind me quietly, then dart across the yard to the opening of the hedge maze. The early morning sun is obscured behind clouds, and the area is covered in fog.

"Gerard?" I half-whisper, half-shout. There is no response.

I step into the maze and let the tugging sensation guide me. Right turn, left turn, right, right. Gerard appears in front of me, startling me.

"Where is she?" I demand, one hand on the gun behind me, the other wrapped around a potion.

"This way," he whispers. He walks just a few more feet, the pulls a long duffel bag out from under the hedge. My stomach unclenches, and a weird relief spreads through me. It reminds me of what I felt when I found Patrick. He unzips it quickly and pushes the edges away.

Inside is—I don't know what. There is a pile of blood-soaked red curls on the thing's head. The face is swollen and misshapen, a long bulbous nose appears broken, and the skin is mottled blue and purple and green.

"Heal her," Gerard says, staring up at me with wide eyes.

Oh god, it's Maybelle. The realization makes me want to vomit.

"Is she even still alive?" I ask as I kneel next to the bag, my hands hovering over her. I don't know where to begin.

"Yes," he hisses, grabbing my hands and pulling them onto her chest.

Maybelle groans and twitches. I shut my eyes to block out the sight in front of me and let my healing magic sink into her.

There are numerous cuts all over her body, and even more bruises. Her nose is broken, she has lost too much blood, and she is slipping in and out of consciousness. I do what I can to steady her heartbeat and pull her back from the edge of shock, but this is completely beyond my skills. The damage is too extensive.

"Lift her head and give her the red and yellow potions that are in my left pocket," I say to Gerard.

He digs the potions out of my pocket, setting the green one aside. He has to pull the bag farther open and tug her shoulders up in order to rest her head on his lap. He tugs her mouth open, revealing a missing tooth, and pours the first potion down her throat, and then the second. She swallows, her eyes flickering open.

"It will help with the pain and the blood loss," I explain.

Maybelle lets out a sigh, and I can feel the pain potion sweeping through her.

"How did you find her?" I ask.

Gerard squints at me. "The Finding magic, it worked. I saw it on the map before you collapsed and burned the whole thing up."

"Why didn't you tell me? I could have helped!" I demand. I should have recognized the strange feeling in my stomach, the constant disquiet. I wish I had someone who could teach me, but instead I'm left bumbling through all of this on my own.

"She wouldn't have wanted you involved," he says, leaning over her head protectively.

I pull my phone out, one hand still on Maybelle's chest, and dial 911.

"What are you doing?" Gerard demands, grabbing for the phone. I lean out of his reach.

"She's dying," I snap. "I'm barely keeping her alive

right now. We have maybe thirty minutes to get her medical attention."

"She's going to hate you for this," Gerard growls.

"At least she'll be alive to do it," I growl back.

"Pecan Grove Police Department, please state your emergency."

17

"No, for the last time, he just showed up at the clanhouse shortly after dawn and asked me to heal her," I say evenly, though my nails are digging into my palms.

Brunson is using this as an opportunity to work off some pent-up aggression by being an asshole. Hawking isn't here to reign him in like she usually does. He has asked me to repeat my story at least five times. He tried to make me tell him what happened in reverse order, and I barely reined in the impulse to kick him in the shin.

It's been four hours since we got to the hospital, and I haven't had any updates on her condition. We're obviously not related, so I'm not sure if I'll get them at all.

"Did Gerard mention how he had found her?" Brunson asks, leaning in.

"No," I say, holding his gaze. I can only hope Gerard will back up my story, I have no idea what he'll do now that I've gotten the police involved.

"Ms. Carter?" A tall nurse with a deep voice and bright purple scrubs is scanning the waiting room from the doorway.

I stand and walk toward him. "That's me."

"She has woken up," he says with a calming smile. "And she is asking for you."

"Thank god," I say, relieved. "Where is her room?"

"I'll take you there."

"I'm coming with you," Brunson says from behind me.

"I'm afraid you'll have to wait, sir," the nurse says. "She requested to speak with Olivia alone first."

Brunson pulls out his badge, and I roll my eyes. "I'm a JHAPI agent, I have a right to— "

"Miss Maybelle is a victim, not a suspect, and per hospital policy, you will have to wait to talk to her until she is ready," the nurse says firmly, his friendly smile fading into a frown of disapproval.

Brunson bristles but doesn't argue further, shoving his badge back into his pocket with jerky motions.

"Now, it's just down this hall," the nurse says, putting his hand on my shoulder and guiding me out of the waiting room.

The hall is empty except for the occasional nurse slipping from room to room. I hate the open doors because I can't help looking, and each person lying inside looks gray and old with all the tubes sticking out of them. When I was younger, I used to sneak into the hospital and try to heal them all a little bit, but it was never enough, and I was left depleted. My mom put a stop to it as soon as she found out.

The nurse stops in front of a closed door. Maybelle's name is scrawled on the little whiteboard, and her doctor's name underneath.

"She looks rough, but she's not in any pain, all right?" he says, his hand on the door handle.

"All right," I say with a nod.

He pushes the door open, and I step into the dim

room. The blinds are drawn, and the only noise is her raspy breaths. I hear the door click shut behind me as I approach the small lump in the bed. She'd be barely four feet tall if she was standing. More than that though, Maybelle always had such a large presence. She seems so diminished here.

I can understand the nurse's warning as well. They cleaned off the blood, and that has only made the cuts more obvious. They crisscross her face and arms, and I imagine they must cover her entire body. I don't understand why anyone would do this to her.

She opens her eyes and squints at me.

"Olivia?"

"Yes." I force myself forward and sit in the chair next to the bed.

"Tell her, Maybelle," Gerard says, materializing out of the shadows.

I jump out of my chair, startled to see him in here.

Maybelle shakes her head, the curls bouncing around her narrow face. The heart monitor blips faster.

"You can tell her, or I will!" Gerard snaps.

"You had no right to force this," Maybelle hisses. "After everything I've done for you."

"I had to! If I hadn't, then we would all have been doomed."

Maybelle scoffs. "You and your premonitions."

"Have I ever been wrong?" Gerard says, baring his teeth back at Maybelle.

"What the hell is going on?" I blurt out finally.

Maybelle goes quiet, still not looking at me.

"Ask her a question, Olivia," Gerard says. "Ask her how she knew your mother."

I stare at Maybelle, eyes wide, my heart in my throat. She isn't speaking, just staring at her hands.

"How—how did you know my mother?" I ask.

A wave of purple magic rolls from her throat to her mouth. Her lips tremble. She sighs heavily and looks up at me. "I knew your mother, years ago."

The magic explains the cuts and bruises all over her body. I feel sick to my stomach; I wouldn't have asked if I had known. She has to answer now, and she has to answer truthfully, or the potion will attack her. It will kill her if she resists too many questions. Whatever the coven that had kidnapped her was asking, she was resisting strongly. No one holds out forever; not many secrets are worth dying to protect.

This explains the missing crystals too. Some of them could have been used to brew a potion like this. I curl my fingers into my palm, hating them for taking something that could be used for good and twisting it like this.

"We weren't friends. More like business partners," she says with a shrug. "She had hired me to procure a few specialty ingredients for her personally, and she was my contact for any work I did for her coven. A couple of years after we started working together, she calls me. Turns out, she's fallen in love with her boyfriend, wants to have a baby with him."

Maybelle shakes her head like she disapproves. "Everybody knows vampires can't have kids, but she's set on it."

She's right. Vampires are undead, kept alive by magic, and can't seem to reproduce. Even if they could, witches can generally only have children with another witch. There's maybe a two percent chance of a successful pregnancy with a human.

"She hired me to find a way. And I did, which, no offense, was the biggest mistake of my life."

My palms begin to sweat, and I can feel Novak's magic getting twitchy inside of me. I should probably sit down, but I'm feeling the urge to run away.

Maybelle picks at the blanket, clearly uncomfortable telling me about any of this.

"I found a way though. For her to have her child. There is an old coven full of some real crazies. They collect magical artifacts, and there were rumors about this spell book that contained the secret to creating a child of a witch and vampire."

I swallow uncomfortably. "Creating something like that would be a bad idea. The vampire and witch councils already hate each other. Something like that would just be a reason to fight."

"Indeed," Maybelle agrees, inclining her head. "Your mother didn't care though. And so, we worked together to steal the book. If she helped, she could use the book to have her baby, and then I would get to sell it and keep all the profits. She agreed."

I want to throw up, but I stare at her instead. I have to hear this; I have to know.

"This coven isn't your normal, run of the mill coven. They're more of a cult, really. They claim to be the guardians of some ancient artifact. No one is really sure what they think they're protecting everyone from, but they hoard power and old magical items. They were the perfect target. We took several things that day, but all they've ever wanted back was that damned book."

Maybelle doesn't continue; simply stares at the floor.

"What happened next?" I ask, knowing the potion will force her to answer. She has to tell me the rest; I can't go the rest of my life wondering. Purple magic crawls up, constricting around her throat.

"It's ugly, Olivia, not the kind of thing you should have to hear about your mother," she says, straining against the tug of the potion.

"Just tell me," I bite out.

She takes a deep breath and looks up again. "They prepared for the spell we found in the book. She had to acquire a few things. Something from each branch of magic, a special brew she made herself, and the stars had to be aligned. As luck would have it, in a few weeks they were. We met in a cabin in the woods to perform the spell."

Maybelle pauses, taking a deep breath, her eyes scanning my face before she continues.

"I waited in another room until I heard her screaming." Maybelle covers her face with her hands for a moment before continuing. "He turned to dust while he was still inside her. Apparently, the magic required a price, one we didn't know about. The book," she shakes her head, "it was not clear. We barely kept in touch after, but I knew the spell worked, and I knew what you were. I went into hiding with my brother, buying both of us a new identity. Gerard watched you throughout the years. He urged me to hire you when you came through town because he insists you are important somehow. And I admit, I have grown fond of you."

Maybelle smiles tremulously for a moment, but the smile falls away at the expression on my face. I stare down at the floor, trying to wrap my head around this. In some ways, it explains everything.

My magic has never been normal. I was born with no magic at all, or so my mother thought until the day after I turned five years old.

I was watching her brew and decided I wanted to be able to brew as well. I had grabbed her arm, and I had *taken*. I can still see her face, the confusion turning to horror, then the scream of pain as I stole her magic. I had stopped as soon as I could, but I was confused, and I was hungry for her magic. She had laid on the floor, unable to move, while I had cried and shaken her shoulders, begging my mom to wake up.

I shake my head, trying to pull myself out of the memories.

"So I'm…" I can't finish the sentence.

"Half-vampire? Yes." She winds her fingers together and shakes her head. "And the people who planted the bombs weren't trying to kill me, they were sending a message. They want to know where the book is. Well, they wanted to."

She pauses, glancing at Gerard, who nods.

"I was not able to fully resist the potion, Olivia, I am sorry," she says quietly.

"What do you mean?" I ask, even though I think I know the answer.

"They know who you are now. They will be coming for you."

"Okay," I say even though it isn't. I run my hands through my hair and pace the small area by the hospital bed. My mind is teeming with questions. I'm not sure I want the answers to all of them, but I feel compelled to ask.

"Who was my father? What was his name?" My mother would never tell me, and now I finally understand why.

"Dominic Bernard," Maybelle says. "I don't remember what clan he was with, but it was not a powerful one."

"The stars will be aligned in the same way again in just a couple of months, but they cannot find the book. I think the cult is desperate," Gerard says. "Leave with us, Olivia. We are going to go into hiding again. We can help keep you away from them."

Running away doesn't sound bad at all. If what I am gets out, and it most likely will with Maybelle under the influence of a truth potion still, I'm screwed. I don't even want to think about how Reilly might react.

"What are you going to tell the JHAPI agents?"

"Nothing," Gerard says. "We're leaving before they will have a chance to question her."

I press the heels of my hands to my eyes. "I need a minute to think. How long do I have, before you leave?"

Gerard shares a look with Maybelle.

"A few hours, at most. We have to leave well before sunset."

I take a step back toward the door. "I'm going to get coffee. I'll be back, just don't— don't leave without me."

"It's not safe for you to go anywhere by yourself," Maybelle objects, but I'm already opening the door and slipping out.

I had always known I was different and that there was something wrong with me. I walk down the hall, fighting the urge to run, barely seeing anything in front of me.

My mother had made such a big deal about me keeping what I could do a secret. I wonder if she ever intended to tell me the truth about what I am.

I slip out of the intensive care unit and hurry toward the elevators. This part of the hospital is busier. The halls are filled with worried families, new parents, and dreary people being pushed along in wheelchairs. I wind my way through them as quickly as I can without breaking out into a jog.

There is, thankfully, no one else waiting for the elevators. I press the button a few times, then watch the floors count steadily up on the left one. I stand a couple of steps back from the doors, arms crossed.

The elevator dings, and the doors open. Hawking steps off, her eyes landing on me immediately.

"Olivia, I was hoping you were still here," Hawking says, "How is she?"

I brush past her without answering and mash the door close button on the elevator without making eye contact.

Her brows pinch together, an expression of pity already forming on her face, and she steps forward.

"Olivia—"

The doors close in her face, and my stomach jerks as the elevator rushes toward the basement parking level. I lean against the wall and cover my face with my hands. I don't know what I should do. Running has always worked for me, sort of.

Zachary's hurt face nags at the back of my head. I had run without a second thought that day, and I've regretted it ever since. I wonder if Patrick would feel as betrayed.

The elevator dings, and the doors slide open. I step into the dimly lit parking garage and pull the keys from my pocket. They hadn't let me ride in the ambulance, so I had borrowed one of Javier's cars.

My footsteps echo loudly as I walk. I'm not sure where I intend on going, but I have to get out of this hospital to think.

I unlock the car and the flicker of the lights illuminate a woman standing near the trunk with her hands clasped. She's about my height, with dark brown hair. The odd part is that she's wearing long white robes.

I stop and stare at her.

"I need you to move, that's my car." My voice seems overly loud in the empty garage.

"Where are you going?" she asks in a girly voice.

"I don't know, just move."

She steps into the light and smiles at me.

"You are special, you know."

"Thanks, I guess," I say, my hand slipping into my jacket pocket for a potion that isn't there. I grit my teeth and sincerely regret my stupidity. I should have just stayed in the room with Gerard and Maybelle.

"You could be trained and given even more magic, Olivia," she says, walking toward me, hands held out to her side as though to show me she isn't holding any weapons. "We could give you anything you wanted."

"I really, really doubt that," I say, taking a step back to keep the space between us. "What the fuck do you want?"

The woman stops, a smile spreading across her face. "We want to help you."

"Help me? Is that why you kidnapped and tortured my friend? Blew up the store we were building together?" I demand, my voice rising with each word.

The smile fades from the woman's face. "She was trying to keep you from your birthright."

I snort. "You know nothing about my birth."

"I know you are the progeny of a vampire and a witch," the woman, says almost worshipfully. "You are a miracle, and you will be our salvation."

"You are insane," I say, taking a step back. "Get away from me and stay away from Maybelle, or I'll hunt you all down and kill you myself."

"You are so stubborn, Olivia. Just like your mother," the woman says with a sigh. She lifts her hand, and wind rushes past my ears, whistling through the parking garage like a freight train.

18

Just like your mother.

Rage boils up in my chest, and the electric magic snaps down into my fingertips. I lift my hand, intending to annihilate her somehow, but a wall of air hits me and flings me backward.

I hit a Suburban, my head snapping back painfully against the window, but I stay conscious. The wind presses against me, impossibly strong. It tugs at my cheeks and whips my hair around my face.

The woman walks forward, one hand out-stretched, not even a hint of effort showing on her face.

"You will come back with us, and you will come to understand your place in all this," she says calmly. "I wish you would come peacefully, but I'm afraid I can't take no for an answer."

"Did you kill my mother?" I ask, struggling to my arms. My voice is barely a whisper over the wind, but I know she heard me. She shakes her head and frowns.

"No, your mother killed herself with her lies," she says, her face twisting into a frown. "We could have found you so much sooner if she hadn't."

Maybelle's bloody face flashes through my mind, and I scream in anger. The pain they must have put my mother through makes me want to kill each and every one of them.

I quit pushing against the wind and simply let set my magic free. A bright orange bolt of lightning darts through the wind. The woman leaps to the side, and the blot strikes where she had been standing, melting the concrete.

I run forward, but another burst of wind hits me from the side. It lifts me from my feet, and I slam down onto the concrete sliding toward another car. Several car alarms go off, the blaring echoing through the parking garage.

I lift my hand from where I'm lying, and the magic surges up from my gut and flies from my fingertips, darting across the space like a lightning bolt. My hair stands on end as the magic strikes twice in quick succession, but the woman leaps out of the way each time.

"You won't hit me, Olivia," the woman says with a tinkling laugh. "But I could teach you how to."

I push myself up into a sitting position, panting as I try to catch my breath. Novak's magic takes so much more out of me than the others.

"Go to hell," I bark at her.

The wind shifts, pushing at me from my left side. I claw at the ground, but there is nothing for me to hold on to. The woman pulls a potion from the pocket of her robe. I don't want to find out what it is.

"Police!" Hawking's voice cuts through the garage, drawing the attention of both of us. She's striding forward, hands held by her sides, fingernails lengthening into claws. "Set the vial down carefully and back away from Olivia."

The woman snorts at Hawking and dismisses her.

"This isn't over."

A growl reverberates the area, followed by the snap of bones as Hawking shifts, her clothes simply ripping off her body as she morphs into a wolf. She howls, a sound that shakes me down to my bones and echoes painfully through the parking garage. It makes me want to run even though I know I'm not the one being hunted.

The witch's face twists into irritation, and she lifts her hand toward Hawking. The wind pushing at me stops suddenly, and I leap at her as Hawking is hit with a rush of wind.

My fist collides with her jaw, shooting pain through my hand. She stumbles back but catches me in the stomach with a kick. The next kick hits my face, and I see stars. My knees hit the floor.

Hawking leaps over me, teeth bared, but the woman is running away. Another push of wind keeps us pinned where we are, sliding slowly away from her. Hawking struggles against it, her head pushed low, but I know there's no point. I'm nauseous and angry and despite my dangerous abilities, unable to kill even one air witch, apparently.

The wind ceases suddenly, and I hear the quick slap of someone running coming from the direction of the elevators. I stay crouched on hands and knees. Hawking licks my face once, then darts off in the direction the woman ran.

Someone kneels next to me, putting their hand on my back. I look up into Brunson's worried face. I jerk away, dislodging his hand, and struggle to my feet.

"Air witch," I gasp. "Go help Hawking."

"Are you okay?"

"I'm fine! Just go!"

Brunson sprints after his partner, gun drawn.

As soon as he gets out of sight, I dash for the elevators. I hit the button several times, but the elevator doesn't open. I give up and run for the stairwell, taking the steps two at a time.

I'm gasping for breath by the time I hit floor three, but I don't stop. My legs burn and my lungs ache, but I make it up the last flight of stairs and burst out of the stairwell. I look around, trying to gain my bearings. A nurse gives me an odd look, but people are frantic in hospitals all the time.

I walk briskly down the hall I think Maybelle's room is in. I scan each door for her name and finally find it. Her door is shut, but I don't bother knocking. I push the door open, then freeze. The room is empty.

"Everything all right?"

I jump, startled, but see it's the same nurse as before, with the purple scrubs.

"Where is she?"

"What are you talking about?" he asks, brows furrowed.

"Maybelle, she's gone," I say, pointing into the room.

He pushes past me and looks into the room. When he turns back, his eyes are wide.

"You said you lost the scent," Brunson argued.

"I did, but if we get Reilly out here, he might be able to catch something I missed," Hawking says, hands on hips, staring Brunson down. "The older vampires can track better than I can. Especially in a well-trafficked area like that."

"I don't think we should involve him this early. I don't trust him," Brunson says, crossing his arms.

Hawking rolls her eyes and huffs. "You don't trust anyone."

"I trust you."

"That took a couple of years," Hawking says, smirking at him, her eyes crinkling around the edges with mirth.

Brunson grins like it's a well-worn conversation, made humorous because of the familiarity.

I rest my elbows on my knees and put my face in my hands. For once, I'm in agreement with Brunson; they should leave Reilly out of it. I'm not about to suggest that though. I also don't think Maybelle and Gerard were kidnapped again. They just fled and left me behind. I guess I deserve this after doing it to other people so many times.

Hawking comes and plops down in the chair next to me, thumbs hooked around her belt buckle. It's a taco today. I wonder if they're all food-themed. She must keep a collection of them in her car with her extra clothes. I had expected her to have to borrow some hospital scrubs after she had busted out of her clothes with her shift, but she had come back up dressed in another suit, gaudy belt buckle in place.

"Did Maybelle say anything about who had taken her?" Hawking asks.

I lean my head back against the wall.

"She said they were insane."

Hawking barks out a laugh. "I think that's a given."

My phone buzzes. I check it absentmindedly, but the message makes my fingers tighten around my phone.

Meet us behind the Full Moon bar in two hours or we leave without you. Come alone.

. . .

"Everything all right?" Hawking asks.

"Yeah, sorry." I try to smile, but I'm sure it looks more like a grimace. "Just Johnny asking how Maybelle is. It'll be hard to break it to him that she's gone again."

Brunson's phone rings, and he answers it and Hawking goes to stand next to him to listen in. I slip my phone back into my pocket and tap my fingers restlessly against my knee.

I could stay. I could help them find the coven that killed my mother and risk everyone finding out what I am, but I don't want to live a life in servitude to the vampire council. Or the witch council. Or be killed by someone afraid I can steal their magic. There's a chance I can find and kill this coven on my own if I get away now. I have to try that first.

I've found the easiest way to sneak away from someone is to make it look like you aren't sneaking away. Walking anywhere with confidence makes it seem like you belong, and it makes people far less likely to question you.

I stand and walk out. Hawking's eyes follow me, but she stays in the room with Brunson. I have two hours to go back to the clanhouse, get Mr. Muffins and anything that might be useful, and get to Full Moon.

I fling the front door open, startling two of the neckers who were about to open the door themselves. One is the girl Patrick had hurt. She looks much brighter now and gives me a big smile as she steps out of my way.

"Hi, Olivia," she says, her accent slightly less thick

now that she isn't nervous.

"Hey…" I realize I don't actually know her name. I don't know most of their names, I've never bothered to ask. It was easier to keep them all at arm's length. I was their healer, not their friend.

"It's Abby," she says with a smirk. "And this is Jackson. He's new too."

The young man next to her extends his hand. He has blond hair and patchy scruff that doesn't suit him. I'm sure that'll be gone in a few days. Emilio has a way of cleaning them all up the first week they're here.

"Nice to meet you, Abby and Jackson," I say, shaking his hand. "I'll see you around."

I start to walk past them, but Abby puts her hand on my arm.

"Could you tell Patrick I'm really not mad next time you see him? He's been avoiding me."

"Sure," I say with a smile that doesn't reach my eyes.

I can't, and the reminder that I'll probably never see Patrick again twists in my gut, but there's nothing I can do about it. I brush past them and race upstairs.

Mr. Muffins looks up when I burst into my room, her tail twitching.

"Time to go," I mutter as I scan the room for the cat cage. It's in the corner under a few dirty towels. I throw the towels on the floor and open the cage door.

Mr. Muffins tenses, butt twitching like she's going to pounce. Her lips curl back, and she hisses at me.

"No," I say, pointing at her sternly. "There is no time for this. We have to leave."

She meows and darts into the bathroom. I run after her and slam the door shut, trapping us both inside. She hates the cat carrier, but I'm not leaving her behind. She can claw me all she wants.

I lunge, arms outstretched, and she jumps into the shower and tries to claw her way up the shower wall. I grab her with two hands, but she somehow twists and gets me with her claws and her teeth at the same time.

"You cranky bitch!" I shout while trying not to squeeze her too hard. Her soft fur makes her slippery, and she's still flailing around, clawing at everything she can reach. I grit my teeth and push the door handle down with my foot, then kick the door open.

I shove her into the cat cage and quickly slam the door shut. She attacks the door once, then curls into the back, growling continuously.

"I know you hate it," I apologize. "But I'm not leaving you behind, okay?"

Her tails whips from side to side, and she hisses at me again.

"Good talk," I say, patting the top of the cage and standing to look around the room. I can get more clothes, all I'm going to take are a few potions. Maybelle may still not be completely healed.

I grab a bag and carefully set the potions inside. I toss a couple of clean shirts in on top as well; they'll work as padding.

The gun Lydia gave me is sitting on the top of the dresser. I consider leaving it, but I may need it. I tuck it into my waistband and pull my shirt over it to hide it.

I hoist the bag onto my shoulder, then pick up Muffin's cage. Her paws poke out the holes in the door, and she meows pitifully.

"I see you have moved on to bargaining. That's not going to work either."

I check my phone. It's been almost an hour since

Gerard texted me. I have another hour to get to them.

I peek my head out into the hall, which is empty. I slip out, kicking the door shut behind me with my foot and hurry toward the stairs. I get halfway down when I hear a knock on the door. I freeze, one foot hovering over the next step.

They knock again, louder this time. Leslie comes from the direction of the kitchen and sees me standing on the stairs, staring at the door. She rolls her eyes.

"You could have answered it," she says, hand already turning the doorknob.

"Leslie, wait!"

She pulls the door open.

A man with white hair and a long beard stands on the front porch, his hands clasped in front of him. He's wearing robes. Black ones with long sleeves and strange symbol embroidered on the chest.

"Can I help you?" she asks.

"Are you Olivia Carter?" he asks, smiling serenely.

"No," Leslie says, crossing her arms.

The man lifts his hand and backhands Leslie. She flies backward and lands limp in the middle of the foyer, her head cracking against the wooden floor.

The man steps inside, his eyes going straight toward me. Wind whistles through the open doorway.

19

I turn and sprint back up the stairs. I don't know where to go, or if there is a way back out from up here, but I can't take two of them. I couldn't even take one of them in the parking garage, and that was with both hands free.

Mr. Muffins is banging around in her cage, partially from me running, but mostly because she's losing her shit. Wind is already whipping up the stairs behind me. I sprint toward my room, no plan other than getting a door between me and them, but the gust catches me around the shoulders and I hit the floor, hard.

The cat cage bounces a foot away, and Mr. Muffins shrieks angrily. The wind stops abruptly, and I scramble toward the cat cage, grabbing it.

A necker bursts out of one of the rooms, hair tousled, wearing yesterday's clothes. I think she's the one I saw Reilly feeding from last time. She opens her mouth to yell at me, but I don't wait for her to speak.

"Run!" I yell at her. "Wake Javier!"

I sprint down the hall, searching frantically for Reilly's room. I have no idea if he's old enough to wake during the day, but I have to try.

I open the door and see him lying in bed, completely unclothed except for a pair of silky boxers that really don't leave much to the imagination. I run to his side, shove Mr. Muffins under the bed, and shake him violently, looking over my shoulder to see if they've found me yet.

"Reilly, wake up, wake up," I whisper harshly.

His eyes twitch, but he doesn't budge. I don't have time to wait for this, and there's only one thing I can think of that might wake him. I pry his mouth open and shove my wrist into it before I can hesitate anymore. His fangs pierce my skin painfully as his jaw clamps down around my wrist.

His eyes fly open, and his hands wrap around my arm. He sucks once, hard, and it makes my knees go weak with a combination of ill-timed pleasure and fear.

"Reilly," I gasp.

He shoves my arm away from him and stares at me, breathing just as hard as I am.

"What are you—"

There's an explosion in the hallway that shakes the entire house.

"Don't make us play hide and seek, Olivia," the woman from the parking garage shouts. "You won't like our technique."

"I don't have time to explain," I say, running toward the door.

Reilly leaps out of bed and follows me, but his movements are slow and stilted.

"I will not be at my usual strength with the sun still up," he says as I put my hand on the doorknob.

"Then just run, get anyone out you can," I say before pulling the door open and stepping out to face this crazy bitch and whoever she has brought with her.

The woman is standing at the end of the hall, a man beside her who looks exactly like her, even down to the length of his hair. They walk in sync toward me, a wide smile on her face, while his expression stays blank. The walls and carpet are scorched, whatever fire damaged them gone now.

A man with a long white beard walks behind them. A sick feeling tears through me. I recognize him from the cafe. I had forgotten it until now, but he bumped into me. He must have set the bombs.

He's wearing a black robe, which he unbuttons and drops to the floor. Underneath is a sleeveless shirt and strange, loose fitting pants that are tight at the ankle. Magic ripples down his arms, and the muscles twist and bulge. A power type, then.

He runs at me. I take a step back, but I won't be able to dodge this. The door next to me swings open, and Reilly steps out, landing a kick in the man's stomach as he gets close. It stops the man in his tracks, but he grabs Reilly and tosses him back toward the stairs.

He turns back to me, but the woman raises her hand.

"Deal with the vampire, we will handle Olivia."

Reilly struggles to his feet and smiles at the bearded man. "You're weak, old man."

"Strong enough to crush you," the man says in a deep, rumbling voice as he charges at Reilly.

I have no time to see what happens next because the witch gets my attention with a rush of wind that forces me to stumble backward.

"You will be coming with us today, Olivia," the woman says. "I'll give you this one chance to come peacefully."

"Like hell I will," I snap. I'm pretty sure I'm screwed, but I'm not going down without a fight.

The two attacking witches step forward in unison, almost as though they are dancing. The moves seem practiced, or at least familiar.

I pull the gun from my waistband and point it at her, but the woman lifts her hands and moves them like she's conducting an orchestra. Wind pummels me from every direction, and I struggle to keep my footing. The gun is ripped from my hands and flies down the hallway.

I send a single burst of electric magic toward her, but she steps out of the way without any effort. She pushes me back farther and farther until I hit the wall. Nowhere to run, no way to stop her.

The wind ceases, and she stares at me like I'm a specimen to be examined.

"The goblin told us everything," she says, walking toward me as I lean against the wall panting.

"Only because you poisoned her," I sneer.

"We can teach you, Olivia," she says earnestly, like I never spoke. "The power you could wield is amazing. You just have to have the courage to take it."

"You are out of your mind," I say, looking between her and her silent twin.

"Here's your first lesson, dodging an offensive attack."

She doesn't move, but her twin does. He lifts a hand and ball of fire hurtles toward my location. I jump to the side, tucking into a roll. Fire smashes into the spot I was just standing, burning through the sheetrock, then disappearing in a flash.

"You were born for a reason, one you don't understand yet, and one your mother and father had no way of knowing when they performed that spell."

Her twin twitches his hand, and another fireball appears out of nowhere, hurtling toward me faster than the last. I dodge again, but just barely. The smell of singed hair fills my nose.

"You could be faster, Olivia," she taunts.

Her brother lifts his hand, and I brace myself to move, but nothing happens. She smirks. I smell something burning and risk glancing behind me but still see nothing.

A breeze pushes my hair against my neck. I leap away from it on instinct, and a pillar of fire shoots down from the ceiling. The carpet curls up from the sheer heat of the fire that is intense even from a few feet away.

"Bravo, Olivia!" She claps in excitement with a bright smile. "Your potential is undeniable."

Her eyes are bright, and the smile on her face seems genuine.

"Why did you kill my mother? Just for stealing your shitty book?" I ask. The question has been weighing on me since she attacked me in the parking garage.

"I already told you, she killed herself. She told lie after lie before we could even ask her a question. She was dead within minutes, and there was nothing we could do to stop it."

"And you bribed someone to fake a death certificate?" I ask, rage building in my chest, the stolen magic sparking along my whole body.

"Yes, we had to end the searching. The case had gone cold. At the time, we thought the detective searching for her was simply trying to earn a promotion or curry favor with her coven. It was simple enough to end it quietly with a little paperwork."

I lift my hands and shove magic at both of them. Pure white crackling bolts of electricity leap from my hands and shoot across the room. The smell of ozone fills my nose.

The twin lifts his hands, and a wall of flame shoots up between us, blocking the magic I've just cast. The electricity spreads out like a net when it hits the wall of flame. The opposing magics twist together in a shower of sparks and fire. I feel the collision down to my bones; it's almost enough to bring me to my knees.

The flames suddenly grow, leaping around the net of electricity. I feel wind on my face. I push, but I don't think I can outlast them, not with both of them working together. I falter just for a moment, but their magic overwhelms mine in that instant. I'm thrown back, my head bouncing off the floor.

Stars spark across my vision, and I feel like I might throw up, but I struggle onto my knees.

"Perhaps you just need us to raise the stakes," the woman says. She nods at her brother, and he kicks in the door next to him. My hearts drops into my stomach as I realize whose room that is.

Her twin walks out, dragging a completely unconscious Patrick by his arm.

"Get away from him," I say, my hands curling into fists and my magic surging up inside of me again. I won't let them hurt him. With shaking legs, I rise to my feet.

"Oh, is this one a friend?" the woman asks, tilting her head. "That makes it so much better."

The twin drops Patrick's arm, and they both step away from him.

"Come and get him, Olivia. See if you can save your friend before Logan turns him to ash."

She lifts her hand, and I sprint toward Patrick. Flames are already rushing toward him, and her twin, Logan, has a strange expression on his face bordering on glee. I reach in my pocket and grab the potion I've been saving for the right moment. This is it.

I wrap my hand around Patrick's arm and throw the potion with my other hand. The vial shatters on the floor right in front of the rushing flames which disappear in a pop, fizzling out with no oxygen to fuel them.

I drag Patrick with me, running backward as fast as I can. Oxygen rushes back into the area, and the flames charge toward us once again. I grit my teeth and raise my hands and *push*. I don't hold anything back.

My magic collides with Logan's once again, but I don't falter this time. The woman's magic joins his, battering against the sparking net of electric magic that is barely holding back the flames. Inch by inch, they push forward. I stand over Patrick, who is still dead asleep, and hold my ground. But I know I won't be able to last forever.

I hear a door open and slow steps. I glance back and see it's Javier. He stumbles down the hall, his eyes half-open, using the wall to support him. He stops directly behind me.

My arms are shaking. My magic is draining out of me like a river while Logan only seems to be growing stronger with his sister feeding the flames.

Javier can barely stand. He won't be able to help; he can't even drag Patrick away.

"Javier, feed me," I gasp out. "I need your magic."

He looks at me, eyes widening.

"Please," I beg. "I can't hold much longer."

Javier squares his shoulder, then bites down on his own wrist.

"Drink...Olivia..." he whispers as she reaches around and holds his wrist in front of my mouth.

I sink my teeth into his wrist and drink. I give into the dark, hungry thing inside of me. The part that has ached for more since the first time I stole magic.

The magic that keeps Javier alive is different from a witch's magic. It's cold and forceful, almost sentient. It's very much like the thing inside of me. I want it.

Lydia must have told him about her suspicions. I'll be upset later, but for now I just want to survive. I pull it inside of me, letting the cold magic curl up around the fading electricity inside of me. I take and I take, wishing I could just rip it from him like I did Novak.

Javier shudders and sags against me. I can see the limits of his power fast approaching. I rip my teeth from his arm before I'm tempted to take even more. Blood drips down my chin, and I lick my lips, aching for every drop.

The electric magic is still wavering, almost completely drained from me, but there is another kind of power surging through me now. I send one last push of magic against the wall of flame, then charge forward.

My legs pump faster than they ever have. Wind whistles past my ears, and it seems like everything slows down around me. The flames move like butterfly wings, lazy and slow, as I run straight through them. The fire witch's face doesn't register shock until I'm already in front of him, my fist connecting with his jaw with a crunch.

His eyes roll back in his head as he flies backward, slamming into a door frame with a loud thunk. His sister screeches and turns on me, but I dart to the side of her gust of wind. I kick her knee, bone popping and cracking as it gives way. She falls to the side, and I punch her in the side of the head. Pain shoots through my hand.

She goes down on one knee but punches me in the stomach. I grunt in pain but block the second punch, catching her wrist.

"There's so much you don't understand," she says, looking up at me with wide eyes.

"I don't care," I say, shoving her back and kicking her in the side of the head. She flops to the ground, unconscious.

Javier is dragging himself across the floor, teeth bared, toward Patrick, who is still lying prone in the hallway. Patrick's eyes are twitching, but he still can't wake up.

I spot the gun the air witch had tossed away from me earlier and grab it. The metal is still hot to the touch. I stand over her, thinking of my mother's laugh, and the way she smiled as she taught me to brew with the magic I had stolen from her.

I could reach down and steal this woman's magic. Turn her inside out and take everything. But I don't want any part of her in me alongside my mother's magic. She is filth in comparison.

I pull the trigger. The sound deafens me as the bullet rips through her head. Her body twitches, and stills. I walk over to her brother, his eyes flutter open just in time to widen as I point the gun at him as well. I barely hear this shot, my ears still ringing from the first.

I walk into the hallway, my blood pumping, my anger and my hunger unsatisfied. The slide is locked back on the gun, it's out of bullets. I drop it and walk toward the stairs when I hear a crash.

Reilly flies into the front door, cracking it on impact. He struggles to his feet, but his movements are sluggish. The sun still hasn't set.

The witch runs forward. Reilly's shoulders are

slumped, and he's blinking like he can't quite see. I could let the witch kill him. I could just run away.

Instead, I dart downstairs, everything slowing again. The bearded man is running at Reilly. I step into his path and punch him in the chest. I feel his sternum crack. He grunts and coughs, blood splattering my face.

I swing again, but he blocks the punch this time. He's insanely strong. Stronger than me still, but I'm faster. I punch over and over again, driving him backward.

He misses a block, and I wrap my hand around his throat. Summoning the last of the electric magic, I send a surge of it through him. His muscles all contract at once, and he falls to the ground, unconscious.

I stand there, panting and shaking, drained. I can't help looking back at Reilly. He's watching me with a smile on his face.

20

He rolls up onto his feet, showing little of the previous exhaustion.

"When Patrick told me you had used Finding magic, I thought he was lying, trying to throw me off with some half-baked plan. Lydia though, she I believed."

"What are you talking about?" My mouth feels strange as I talk. Something sharp pricks at the inside of my mouth. I prod it gently with my tongue and find a fang. Smaller than a vampire's, but definitely there.

I dig my nails into my palm to keep from reacting, but I'm sure my heart is going crazy. I can almost hear it.

"The welts on your arm. The way you found Patrick when no one else could, and Aaron Hall turns up unable to cast the simplest of Finding spells." He stalks toward me, the glow of the sun setting in a riot of reds and oranges visible through the windows behind him. "The electric magic that sparks on your fingertips every time you get angry."

I step backward, edging around the bearded man's prone figure.

"The healing magic was the first hint. As soon as I started paying attention, the rest became so, painfully, obvious," Reilly finishes with a smile that makes heat stir in my gut and fear twist in my chest. I am one hundred percent fucked.

"So what now, you're going to drag me to the council? Or are you just going to kill me?" My muscles tense, ready for the slightest move even though I know he's far too fast for me to defend against.

"Not the council, not yet. My sire will meet you first."

Reilly crouches down by the bearded man, takes his head and twists. His necks cracks sickeningly as it breaks.

"Why did you kill him? We could have questioned him—"

"He was a loose end," Reilly says, wiping his hands on his pants as he stands. "You're mine now, Olivia. I don't want anyone else knowing what you can do until I am ready."

"I'm not going anywhere with you," I bite out, my hands shaking at my side. "I'll die first."

It's barely dawn, Reilly could still be weak. I shift on my feet, trying to decide if I can move fast enough to kill him. I blink, and he is pushing me back against the wall, his body warm against mine and face inches away. He wraps his hands around my wrists and holds me still.

"You can't kill me, Olivia," he breathes. "If you try, I'll make sure you regret it."

"I doubt that," I growl at him, struggling against his grip. Javier's power is still pulsing through me, but all my other magic is drained.

Reilly grins, all teeth. "You will cooperate, or I will kill every single member of this clan, down to the last necker."

Over his shoulder, I see Patrick standing on the top of the stairs, tears slipping out of his eyes. He mouths, *I'm sorry*, and slips back down the hallway.

I had hoped I would never live to see this day come. Every warning my mother gave me is ringing in my head. I can almost see her out of the corner of my eye, saying, *I told you so*. I let people get too close. I let them see too much.

I have to find a way to get away from Reilly, and I will. Even if it means killing him. It will be hard though, especially with the lives of everyone I care about hanging in the balance. Anger at them, and at myself, is swirling through me. I don't know how to feel, but I know I'm not willing to let them die, even if they have betrayed me. I should have run while I could.

Reilly steps away from me, but I stay pressed against the wall.

"Pack enough for a week. We're leaving early. I'll have Javier send the rest of your things to my clanhouse."

Brunson and Hawking burst into the house, guns drawn. They take in the destruction. Leslie's too still body, and the bearded man lying in the foyer.

"There are two more bodies upstairs. They're part of some kind of cult," I say hoarsely.

Hawking holsters her gun and sprints upstairs. Brunson hesitates, eyes flicking between me and Reilly.

"Everything all right?" he asks, finger on the trigger of his gun.

Zachary knows me well, too well I suppose. He senses the tension that Hawking didn't. Reilly looks back at me, and I know there's only one answer I can give that won't result in Zachary's death. I've been wrong a lot recently, but I was right about one thing. Reilly did find a way to steal my soul.

"Everything's fine," I say, gesturing to the chaos around us. "Just peachy."

Brunson huffs out a chuckle. "I see your point."

I can hear Hawking talking upstairs, saying something to Javier in soothing tones. I look up, brows pinched together. I shouldn't be able to hear that. I guess I took more from Javier than just speed and strength.

"Did they say if they had taken Maybelle again?" Brunson asks.

"They didn't," I say, lifting my shoulder in a half-shrug. "She and Gerard ran away. They asked me to go with them, but I couldn't get to them in time."

"You were going to run?" Brunson asks confused. "Why?"

I wrap my arms around myself. "They were obviously targeting me. I just wanted to keep everyone out of harm's way."

"You could have told someone!" Brunson says, voice rising, but not quite to a shout as he shoves his gun back into the holster on his side. "We could have helped you, or even prevented this."

Javier chooses that moment to walk downstairs, followed closely by Hawking. He heads straight for Leslie, ignoring us. He scoops her up, careful to support her head, then turns to Reilly.

"Will you help me turn her?"

The room quiets as we all look to Reilly for his response.

"If I do, she must return to my clan. I will be her sire."

Javier nods, but his face falls. He cared for Leslie, depended on her. I know this is my fault. If I hadn't taken so much, he could have turned her himself.

Reilly walks toward the parlor, motioning for Javier to follow. Hawking, Brunson, and I stay in the foyer. Watching would feel like intruding.

"I need to call this in," Hawking says.

Brunson nods. "Go ahead."

Hawking steps outside, phone to her ear.

Brunson looks at me.

"I know it isn't much comfort right now, but we have solid information on Martinez. We can find the rest of this cult too. We won't let this happen again."

He's so earnest, just like the Zachary I knew growing up.

"Reilly said I'd be helping with some raids. Where are we going first?"

"Arizona."

The land of cactus, desert, and scorpions.

"Sounds great," I mutter, slipping down the wall.

I can still feel Reilly's hands around my wrists, trapping me. I rub at them, but there's no escaping the shit I've gotten myself into. Not this time.

MESSAGE TO THE READER

Thank you so much for buying my book. I really hope you have enjoyed the story as much as I did writing it. Being an author is not an easy task, so your support means a lot to me. I do my best to make sure books come out error free.

However, I am the worst with commas. They are my nemesis. I deeply apologize if my comma usage bothered you. Going forward, I am hiring a professional editor to review the books before publication. Eventually, I will be able to have previously published books edited as well. If you found any errors, please feel free to reach out to me so I can correct them!

Reviews are very important to indie authors, and help other readers that would be interested in a series like this find it. I also love reading your thoughts on the book.

To review the book simply go to the website below.

https://readerlinks.com/mybooks/764/1/1237

Follow Me

Thank you so much for buying my book. I really hope you have enjoyed the story as much as I did writing it. Being an author is not an easy task, so your support means a lot to me. I do my best to make sure books come out error free. However, if you found any errors, please feel free to reach out to me so I can correct them!

If you loved this book, the best way to find out about new releases and updates is to join my Facebook group, The Foxehole. Amazon does a very poor job about notifying readers of new book releases. Joining the group can be an alternative to newsletters if you feel your inbox is getting a little crowded.

Facebook Group:
https://www.facebook.com/groups/TheFoxehole
Goodreads:
http://goodreads.com/Stephanie_Foxe
BookBub:
https://www.bookbub.com/authors/stephanie-foxe

Witch's Bite Series (Now complete!)

Borrowed Magic - Book One

Price of Magic - Book Two

Blood Magic - Book Three

Forbidden Magic - Book Four

Misfit's Series

Misfit Pack

Misfit Angel

Misfit Fortune

A new world of magic awaits!

Misfit Pack is the first book in a new series by Stephanie Foxe –

Everything changed in a flash of pain and blood.

All because she had to play hero.

Amber finds herself tied to two strangers, her humanity stripped from her, and a heavy responsibility laid on her shoulders.

Haunted by guilt and loss, she struggles to understand what it means to be a werewolf – and an alpha.

Magic is commonplace, but there is a divide between humans and supernaturals. There are rules. Expectations.

The title of alpha isn't given lightly, it's earned through a

Trial that will test her in ways she never expected.

Left with no choice but to fight for her new status as alpha, Amber must pull together her fledgling pack of werewolves that never wanted to be more than human. Time is ticking as they prepare for the night that could tear them apart. If Amber fails the Alpha Trials, they'll lose a lot more than their humanity.

They'll lose their freedom.

www.stephaniefoxe.com